I0692655

THE DAY OF UNITING

The Novels of
EDGAR WALLACE

THE DAY OF UNITING

BY

EDGAR WALLACE

THE MYSTERY LEAGUE, INC.
PUBLISHERS 1930 NEW YORK

COPYRIGHT, 1921–1930 BY

EDGAR WALLACE

ALL RIGHTS RESERVED
PRINTED IN THE UNITED STATES
OF AMERICA

FIRST EDITION

PROLOGUE

.

PROLOGUE

BY THE side of a printer's steel table, a young man was working busily with tweezers and awl. A page of type neatly bound about with twine was the subject of his attention, and although his hand was shaky and he was, for reasons of expediency, working with only one of the two hundred lights which illuminated the "book-room" of Ponters', he made no mistake. Once he raised his head and listened. There was no other sound than the clacketty-clack of a linotype on the floor below, where the night shift was "setting up" a Sunday newspaper; and as a background to this clatter, the low rumble of the presses in the basement.

He wiped his streaming forehead, and bending lower over the page, worked with incredible rapidity.

He was a man of twenty-three or twenty-four. His face was a little puffy, and his eyes were dull. Tom Elmers liked his cups a little too well, and since that day when Delia Sennett had told him, in her quiet, earnest way, that she had other plans than those he suggested with such vehemence, he had not attempted to check the craving.

Again he raised his head and listened, putting one hand up to the key of the hanging light, in readiness to switch it out, but there was no sound of footsteps on the stone corridor without, and he resumed his work.

So engrossed was he, that when the interruption came he was not aware of another presence in the room, and yet he should have remembered that when Joe Sennett was on night work he invariably wore felt slippers, and should have known that the swing-door was practically noiseless in operation.

Old Joe Sennett, master printer to the firm of Ponters Limited, stood with his back to the door, looking in amazement at the solitary workman. Then he came softly across the floor, and stood at the other's elbow.

"What are you doing?" asked Sennett suddenly, and the man dropped his awl with a little cry and looked around.

"I didn't hear you come in," he gasped.

"What are you doing?" asked Sennett again, fixing those china-blue eyes of his upon the young man.

"I remembered those corrections I had to make. I didn't get them down until just before we knocked off, and they were worrying me, Mr. Sennett."

"So you came back on Saturday night to do them?" said the other dryly. "Well, you're a model workman, Tom."

The man gathered up his tools, and slipped them into his waistcoat pocket.

"A model workman," repeated the other. "I'd like to know why you came back, Tom."

"I've told you, haven't I?" growled Elmers, as he put on his coat.

Joe Sennett looked at him suspiciously.

"All right," he said, "you can clear out now, and don't do it again. If you haven't time to finish your work, leave it."

Near the entrance was a yellow painted iron door marked "Private." It was towards this that Joe went. He stopped to switch on three pilot lights that gave the room sufficient illumination to allow him to move with-

out risk of damage, and then, taking a key
from his pocket, he inserted it. The light
pressure he exercised was sufficient to send
the door ajar. He turned in a flash.

"Have you been to this room?" he asked
sternly.

"No, Mr. Sennett."

Joe pushed open the door and switched on
another light. He was in a small case-room,
which was also equipped with a hand-press.
It was the holy of holies of Ponters' vast
establishment, for in that chamber two trust-
worthy compositors, one of whom was Joe
Sennett, set up those secret documents which
the Government, from time to time, found it
necessary to print and circulate.

"Who opened the door?"

"I don't know, Mr. Sennett."

Joe walked into the room and looked
around. Then he turned.

"If I thought it was you, Tom, do you
know what I'd do with you?"

"What's the use of threatening me?" said
the young man sullenly. "I've had enough
trouble with you already. Delia's put you
against me."

"I don't want you to mention Delia's name to me, Tom," said Joe Sennett sharply.

He lifted a warning finger.

"You're going the right way to get into bad trouble, Tom Elmers. For the sake of your father, who was a friend of mine, I'd like to save you from your own folly, but you're one of the clever kind that'll never be saved."

"I don't want any saving, either," growled Elmers, and the old man shook his head.

"You're keeping bad company. I saw you in the High Street the other night with that man Palythorpe."

"Well, what about it?" asked the other, defiantly. "He's a gentleman, is Mr. Palythorpe. He could buy up you and me a hundred times over. And he's a newspaper proprietor, too——"

Joe chuckled in spite of his annoyance.

"Mr. Palythorpe is an ex-convict who served ten years for blackmailing Mr. Chapelle's daughter. You know that. If you don't, you ought to."

Tom shuffled uneasily. He had been somewhat disconcerted to learn that his friendship with a man of doubtful antecedents was so well known.

"He was innocent," he said a little lamely, feeling that he must justify himself at any rate.

"Dartmoor is full of people who are innocent," said Joe. "Now, Tom, you're not a bad boy," he said in a more kindly voice, "but you've got to keep away from that sort of trash. He could give you a job, I daresay. He's running a paper now, isn't he? But it's not the kind of job that's going to get you anywhere, except into the cell which he has just left."

He jerked his head in sign of dismissal, and Tom, without a word, pushed through the swing-doors and disappeared.

Old Joe paced the length of the big room —it occupied the whole of the floor, and "room" was a ridiculously inadequate description—his hands behind his back, speculating upon the reason for Tom Elmers' sudden industry. His own impression was that the surprise of Elmers was simulated and that he had heard the master printer coming and had busied himself with a page of type in order to hide his real occupation.

Joe looked carefully at every case as he passed, switching on the local lights for the purpose of his scrutiny.

Ponters were the biggest printers in the kingdom, and from their book-room went forth a good proportion of the educational works which were published every year. Here men of all nations worked. French, German, Japanese, and Chinese, for the publishing business of Ponters had a world-wide clientèle.

He finished his inspection and went back to what was known as the Secret Press Room, and settled himself down for the night to put into print a very important memorandum which had been issued that morning by the First Lord of the Admiralty.

But the thought of Tom and his visit constantly intruded. It was true that Palythorpe was an undesirable acquaintance for any honest man. He had been the proprietor of a scurrilous little sheet, which enjoyed a semi-private circulation—it was sent out to its subscribers in envelopes—and he had utilized the paper for the collection of information which might be, and was, extremely useful and profitable to him. The paper was called *Spice,* and it purported to deal in a flippant manner with the dealings of high Society, enjoying in consequence a circulation in certain basement kitchens of Mayfair.

Because he offered generous payment for news about the doings of Society people, Mr. Palythorpe had gathered about him a staff of correspondents ranging from valets to tweeny-maids, who sent him, in addition to such items as were put into print, news that he could not publish, but could embody in letters written under an assumed name; and, being addressed to the subjects of these paragraphs, might produce results which were at once lucrative and satisfactory.

Family scandals, the pitiful little tragedies which break and mar the lives of ordinary men and women, indiscreet letters left about by their careless recipients, these were the marketable commodities which gained for Mr. Palythorpe a handsome income, and might have continued, had he not made the mistake of attempting to blackmail a foolish girl, whose father was the cleverest lawyer of the day. A bad companion for the susceptible Tom Elmers.

"Palythorpe and Tom between them are going to give me trouble," said Joe aloud.

But his prophecy was only realized in part. Mr. Palythorpe himself had small responsibility for the events which sent three men to their graves, and made the hair of Jimmy Blake go white, not in a night, but in one stormy afternoon on Salisbury Plain.

CHAPTER ONE

To JIMMY BLAKE, mathematics were as the Greek of Socrates to the unlearned senator. As for the calculii, they would have filled him with awe and wonder, if he had had any idea of their functions.

When, in the days of his extreme youth, Jimmy had been asked to prove that a circle was equal in area to a triangle whose base was equal to the circumference, and whose height was equal to the radius of the circle, Jimmy magnanimously accepted his master's word that it was so, and passed on to something more human. Though by some extraordinary means he scraped through school with a certificate and emerged from Oxford with a sort of degree, his mathematical paper would have caused Archimedes to turn in his grave.

It was his fate to live in the closest contact with the scientific mind. Jimmy Blake was a rich man and by some accounted eccentric, though the beginning and end of his eccentricity were to be found in his dislike for work and his choice of Blackheath as a desirable residential quarter. He had inherited from his father a beautiful old Georgian house, facing the Heath, and which an enterprising auctioneer would have truthfully described as "standing in extensive and parklike grounds."

Such an agent might have gone on to rhapsodize over the old world gardens of Blake's Priory, the comfort of the accommodation, the Adams' decorations; and when he had exhausted its æsthetic and sylvan charms, his utilitarian mind would probably have descended to such mundane advantages as the central heating, electric installation and the character of the soil on which it stood.

Within these grounds there had once been a veritable priory. At some period of the seventeenth century when Greenwich and Blackheath were fashionable rendezvous for the élite and fashion of Elizabeth's court and when the stately palace by the river saw Raleigh and Leicester, and the grand gentlemen and dames of society strolling on the grassy slopes of the Royal Park, a Major Blake had acquired the property and had erected a pleasure house for himself and his friends. The house no longer existed, but the gardens he had planned still sent forth their ancient fragrance.

To Jimmy the Priory was home, and, though he maintained a modest flat at the back of Park Lane, he spent very little of his time there. The glories of Elizabeth's Greenwich had departed definitely and completely and were one with the Court of Jamshid. Aged pensioners shuffled along the marble halls where the bucks of the Virgin had pranced and prinked, and a heavy-footed Drake had stalked with news of victories on the Spanish Main. Incidentally, Jimmy came from a long line of adventurers and could trace his descent from an uncle of the great Blake.

"It is a standing wonder to me, Jimmy," said Van Roon one night, "why a man like you, with the blood of filibusters in your veins, should be content to loaf through life behind the steering wheel of a Rolls, having no other objective than the satisfaction of your unscientific curiosity."

"No curiosity is unscientific," said Jimmy lazily. "I'm surprised at you, Jerry! Didn't Huxley or one of those Johnnies say——"

Van Roon groaned. His was the scientific mind, against which Jimmy's intelligence was for ever rubbing. Gerald Van Roon was Jimmy's cousin, a brilliant genius to whom the world was a great laboratory, alternating with a small bedroom, with the furnishing of which he had never become acquainted, because he had not remained in the room long enough.

A tall, angular man with large bony hands, a big bulging forehead, two small deep-set eyes which even his immense and powerful spectacles did not magnify, Gerald Van Roon seemed the least suitable of companions for a man of Jimmy's tastes. He was exact, precise, orderly, had no human interests and absolutely no tastes in common with his happy-go-lucky cousin. And yet to the surprise of all who knew them, they lived together in the greatest harmony. Gerald amused Jimmy in one way and impressed him in another. The

man's high principles, his almost fanatical
passion for the truth, which is after all the
basic layer of the scientific mind, his child-
like innocence in all worldly matters, his contempt for commerce and the rewards which
commercial success brings, his extraordinary
idealism—all these were very endearing qualities, which appealed strongly to the younger
man.

"You're a funny devil," said Jimmy, throwing his serviette in a heap on the table. (Gerald Van Roon rolled his precisely and fitted
the napkin ring exactly over the centre of the
roll.)   "I suppose you're going to that stink-
shop of yours?"

"I'm going to the laboratory," said Gerald,
with a faint smile.

"Good Lord!" said Jimmy, shaking his
head in wonder. "On a gorgeous day like
this! Come with me to the sea, Jerry. I've
got the old roller at the door, and in an hour
and a half we'll be on the Sussex Downs,
sniffing the beautiful ozone and watching the
baa-lambs frisk and gambol."

"Come to my lab., and I'll make you some
ozone in two seconds," said Gerald, getting

up from the table and fumbling for his
pipe.

Jimmy groaned. His companion was at
the door when he turned, his hand upon the
handle.

"Jimmy, would you like to meet the Prime
Minister?" he asked.

"Good Lord, no," said Jimmy, astonished.
"Why should I want to meet the Prime Minister. I loathe his politics and I thought the
speech he made the other day about the ty-
ranny of the farmers was in shocking bad
taste."

Gerald frowned.

"Oh, did he make a speech?" he asked in
a vague, surprised tone, as though he had
heard of some abnormality on the part of
the Prime Minister of England. "I never
read speeches, and of course it really doesn't
matter what politicians say—they mean
nothing."

"Why do you want me to meet the Prime
Minister?"

"I don't really want you to meet him," said
Gerald, "but I thought you would enjoy the
experience. Chapelle is very strong for

science and he is really an excellent mathematician."

"I gathered that from his last budget," said
Jimmy grimly, for the Prime Minister was
also Chancellor of the Exchequer.

He saw the puzzled look on Van Roon's
face.

"A budget," he explained politely, "is an
apology made by a responsible minister in
the House of Commons for the robberies he
intends to commit in the ensuing year. But
what about his mathematical qualities? I
have no wish to meet mathematicians. Don't
you think the scientific atmosphere in which
I live is sufficiently thick without introduc-
ing a new brand of fog?"

"It doesn't matter," said Gerald, opening
the door. "Only he's giving a luncheon to
a few interesting people."

"Including yourself?"

"Including myself," said Gerald gravely.
"It is a luncheon party to meet Maggerson.
He's coming back from America, but I sup-
post you know that?"

"Maggerson?" said Jimmy. "Who is
Maggerson?"

If an actor were asked, "Who was Henry Irving?" or a doctor, "Who was Lister?" the questions would produce exactly the same tragic look of incredulity as that which dawned upon the ungainly face of Gerald Van Roon.

"Who is Maggerson?" he repeated. "You're joking, Jimmy."

"I'm not," said Jimmy stoutly.

"Of course you are."

"Who is Maggerson?" demanded Jimmy again, and Gerald walked slowly back into the room and stared down at the unabashed young man.

"You'll ask who Leibnitz was next," he said.

"Oh, I know all about him," said Jimmy confidently. "He was a German socialist who was executed——"

"Leibnitz," interrupted the other severely, "was the greatest mathematician Germany has produced. He was a contemporary of Newton, and together they produced the calculus."

"Good luck to 'em," said Jimmy. "And when they produced it, what did they do with it? Anyway, what is a calculus? Isn't that a sort of multiplication table?"

Here Archimedes must have positively revolved.

Then Jimmy heard about Maggerson and the calculus he had discovered, or invented, or adopted—he was not certain which. It was the calculus which was accepted by all authorities and which had superseded Leibnitz and Newton's and Lagrange's, and was known as "Maggerson's Calculus of Variation."

"Is it a book?" asked Jimmy at last, "because, dear old thing, I'll buy it and read it up. I should hate to meet Mr. Maggerson and not be able to tell him how his little story ends."

Whereupon Gerald Van Roon, realizing that he was against an unreceptive mind, wandered from the room, making gestures of despair and amazement.

There were lots of things that Jimmy had learnt at school and at the University which he had contrived successfully to forget. It was his proud boast that the only definite fact about English literature which remained with him was that Chaucer drank beer at the Tabard Inn. Jimmy had drunk beer at the same inn, though it had been slightly renovated since the days of the Canterbury Pilgrims. It is equally true that he had not only forgotten all that he ever knew about mathematics, but that even the algebraical signs were as foolishly uninformative to him as they had been when he had first met them in a preparatory school.

On the road to Eastbourne he fell in with another young man, who was driving a big Italia car to the common danger of the public. They met after the young man had passed him in a cloud of dust, furiously hooting for passage room. They might not have come into contact with one another at all, but ahead was a police trap into which the furious driver fell.

Jimmy slowed his car when his experienced eye detected a number of the Sussex constabulary concealed in the hedge, and, coming up with the offender, he recognized in him the gilded son of John Ponter, Printer to the King's Most Excellent Majesty.

"Hello, Jimmy," said Ferdinand. "Lo!

Yes?" this to the constable, who was taking laborious particulars in a small notebook. "I live at Carlton House Mansions. Can't this thing be settled out of court, cheery old fellow?"

"It can't, sir," said the representative of the law with some firmness. "You were going fifty-five miles an hour on that road and we've been having accidents here."

"Am I the first accident you've had to-day?" asked Ferdie Ponter, and the constable grinned.

"Stop at the Chequers Inn. It's about a mile along the road," yelled Ferdie as Blake went on. Jimmy waved his hand affirmatively.

At the Chequers they parked their cars and went into the stuffy little bar to drink beer.

"I shall lose my licence this time," said Ferdie gloomily.

"Better lose your licence than lose your young life," said Jimmy. "Where are you going in such a devil of a hurry, anyway?"

"I'm lunching with a little girl at Eastbourne," said Ferdie, and then of a sudden

Jimmy struck the zinc bar against which he was leaning.

"Ferdie, your people do a tremendous lot of scientific printing, don't they?"

"I believe so," said Ferdie. "I never go into the beastly works if I can help it. We've an awfully clever foreman, a man named Sennett."

"Sennett," repeated Jimmy thoughtfully. "Is he an oldish gentleman, rather like Mark Twain in appearance?"

"I never met Mark Twain," confessed Ferdinand, gulping at his beer.

"I know the old boy. He comes to see Gerald with proofs of books and things."

"That's the chap. We print and publish all Van Roon's books, and devilish dry they are," said Ferdie. "Another tankard of nut-brown ale, good dame," this to the brass-haired lady behind the counter.

"Ferdie, what is a calculus?"

"What?" said the puzzled Ferdinand.

"What is a calculus? I've got an idea I know," said Jimmy, "but I can't exactly place the fellow. I'm going to meet a man who's rather a whale on the subject."

"Calculus? I seem to remember something about it," said Ferdinand, scratching
his nose. "Isn't that the mock they used to
teach us at school? A sort of thing for calculating distances and speeds, revolutions and
things? Why? You're not going in for that
sort of tommy rot, are you?"

Jimmy, with a tankard at his lips, shook
his head.

"No, only I'm meeting this fellow Maggerson——"

"Oh, Maggerson? We print him too,"
said the honorary printer. "A wild looking
Johnnie like Paderewski, though I don't
think he plays the piano. As a matter of fact,
we make a lot of money out of him."

He wiped his mouth with a silk handker-
chief and strode out of the bar, and Jimmy,
paying the score, followed. And there and
then might have ended his feeble interest in
the calculus of Mr. Walter Maggerson, but
for the fact that when he got back to Blackheath in time to change for dinner he discovered that Van Roon had two visitors. Steele,
his valet, who was the information bureau of
Blake's Priory, supplied the intelligence.

"Mr. Van Roon's compliments, sir, and will you not dress for dinner to-night, because he has two people whom he must ask to stay, and they are not dressed?"

"Certainly, Moses," said Jimmy. "Put out the suit I wear when I'm not dressed—who are the gentlemen?"

"There's a gentleman and a lady, sir. Well, she's not exactly a lady," he added; "a young girl, if I might describe her so."

"If she looks like a young girl, she probably is, Moses, so there is no great danger of your over-stating the case," said Jimmy.

A few minutes later Gerald came into his dressing-room.

"Do you mind if I ask two people to stay to dinner to-night, Jimmy?" he demanded.

"Of course not," said Jimmy, a little surprised, for his cousin did not usually apologize for his invitations.

"The fact is," Gerald hesitated, "something has gone wrong with that book of mine and Ponters, the printers, have sent down their foreman. You remember him, old Sennett!"

"Sennett?" said Jimmy in surprise. "I was

talking about him to-day. What has happened?"

"I hardly know," said Gerald, "but apparently some scamp at the works, out of sheer mischief, has been interpolating all sorts of ridiculous sentences and statements in the scientific works which Ponters publish. They have only recently discovered this, and one of the first books that seems to have been tampered with was my book on 'The Distribution of Living Forms.' "

"What's that about?" asked Jimmy, interested. "It sounds like a text-book on beauty choruses to me."

"Do you mind if they stay?" asked the other, ignoring the flippancy.

"Not a bit. Of course I don't mind. What is the girl like?"

"The girl?" Jerry rubbed his chin absently. "Oh, she's—er—a girl. She has rather a perfect jaw. I was very much struck by her jaw."

"Is she pretty? I suppose I needn't ask that if you were very much struck by her jaw," said Jimmy.

"Pretty?" Gerald looked out of the window. "I suppose she may be considered pretty. She isn't malformed in any way."

"You're inhuman," said Jimmy hopelessly. "Get out before you corrupt Moses!"

"The fact is"—Gerald was obviously nervous—"I might have to keep Mr. Sennett here till quite late, going through these proofs. Would you mind driving the girl home? Of course, we could telephone for a taxi, but her father is rather nervous about her and I think somebody should accompany her."

Jimmy smiled.

"Anything in the sacred cause of science," he said solemnly.

CHAPTER TWO

JIMMY BLAKE was twenty-seven, above medium height, lean of build and of the athletic type which keen tennis produces and which the war hardened and aged a little. There were lines on his thin brown face which men of twenty-seven do not usually carry, but Jimmy had spent three years behind the controls of a fighting plane, and the wings of the Dark Angel had brushed his cheek a dozen times and had departed. The reaction from the hard realities of war had not found expression in a way which is painfully usual. He had fled from the rigours of war to the lazy, go-as-you-please life which a moneyed man could afford. He was a wholesome normal youth, with a wholesome normal respect for his fellows, be they men or women; but he was the stuff from which confirmed bachelors are made and the prospect of spending an evening with the daughter of a master printer neither alarmed nor pleased him.

He went down to dinner when the gong sounded and found the party already at the table, which was Gerald's way. He recognized immediately the white-haired, white-moustached printer, and then he turned his eyes to the girl who sat at Gerald's right hand. And here he had his first pleasant shock. Remembering Sennett's age, he expected a woman of thirty-five and pictured her a little stout and a little awkward.

But this girl could not have been more than twenty-two. She was petite and dainty, and dressed with delightful simplicity—the kind of dress that every man admires and so few women have the courage to wear. Her face was delicately moulded, the type that Paul Veronese painted from his inner consciousness. The eyes were a deep blue, almost violet, and when they looked up at him gravely, enquiringly, he experienced a queer and not an unpleasant thrill.

"This is Mr. Blake," introduced Gerald. "This is Miss Sennett, Jimmy. You know her father."

Jimmy shook hands with both and sat down

slowly. He could not take his eyes from the girl's face. She fascinated him, though why he could not understand, for he had met many beautiful women, women more stately and more impressive than she, and they had left him cold. She neither flushed nor grew embarrassed under a stare which she might reasonably have regarded as offensive; and Jimmy, recognizing his lapse of manners, turned his attention to the father.

"I was with young Ponter to-day," said Jimmy.

Mr. Sennett did not seem impressed, and the young man gathered that the heir to Ponters' publishing house was not regarded as an admirable member of society.

Jimmy could never recall what they talked about, Delia and he. Her name was Bedelia, and she had been christened in the days when Bedelia was really a pretty name and before it had been promoted by the ragtime song-writer to its present-day notoriety.

Gerald and Sennett were of course absorbed in the book. Old Sennett was, like most printers, a brilliantly knowledgeable man, for the printing trade represents the aristocracy of intellect. He was interesting too in another way. He told stories of work done in the locked room where Government minutes are printed and which only he and another man occupied in the dark days of the war, when the Cabinet secrets he "set" might have been sold to the enemy for fabulous sums.

Gerald and the old man went off to Van Roon's study.

"Now, I'm afraid you're going to be bored," said Jimmy as he showed Delia to the drawing-room. "I can't play or sing or do anything clever—I can't even give you a selection on the Maggerson calculus!"

Delia Sennett smiled.

"He's a very wonderful man, Mr. Blake," she said, and he stared at her.

"Don't tell me you're a mathematician too," he gasped, and she laughed. She had a sweet, low, musical laugh which was music indeed to Jimmy's ears.

"I know nothing about it," said Delia, "and I've been scared to death lest you were as clever as Mr. Van Roon. He's a relation of yours, isn't he?"

Jimmy nodded.

"His mother was my mother's sister. She married a Dutch scientist, or rather a scientist with a Dutch name," he explained. "Jerry and I have lived together in this house since we were kids and you're quite right about his being clever, and equally discerning when you discovered I was not."

"I didn't think you were very keen on scientific subjects," she corrected.

"And I'm not," said Jimmy. "Are you?"

She shook her head. He tried to keep the conversation on the personal note, but he observed she was uneasy and glanced at her watch.

"By Jove!" he said, suddenly jumping up. "I promised to see you home. Are you in any hurry?"

"I want to be home before ten," she said. "I have a lesson to give at eight o'clock tomorrow morning."

She smiled at his look of astonishment.

"I am a teacher of languages," she said; "perhaps I don't look as intelligent as that?"

He protested.

"That's why I am interested in Mr. Van

Roon," she went on. "Dutch and German are my two best languages. It was awfully disappointing to discover that he was so English."

Jimmy chuckled.

"That's where you fall down in your analysis, Miss Sennett," he said. "Jerry talks English, but thinks Dutch! The most terrible thing he does is to make all his notes in shorthand and in Dutch! How does that strike you for a complicated procedure?"

"Do you know Mr. Maggerson?" she asked a little while later, after he had telephoned to the garage for the car and she was making preparations to depart.

"I'm the only man in the world who doesn't," said Jimmy. "It is queer how greatness can exist right under your nose without your being aware of the fact. Do you know him?"

She shook her head.

"Daddy knows him well," she said.

"What is wrong with Jerry's proofs?" he asked, and she was silent. He thought she did not know, but she undeceived him.

"He has been the victim of a very mean

and contemptible action directed against my father," she said with unexpected vigour. "Father is responsible that every book which goes out of Ponters' is typographically accurate. Daddy's firm print all the big scientific books, including Mr. Maggerson's; and Daddy has got a bad enemy, a man whom he helped and who has no reason to hate him— oh, it was mean, mean!"

Jimmy speculated as to the character of the meanness and who was the unfortunate man who had called the flush to Bedelia's face and that bright hard look to her eyes.

She went to the study to say good-night to her father and Jimmy waited on the porch. Presently the car came purring down the drive and stopped before him.

"It's all right, Jones," said Jimmy as the chauffeur got down; "I shan't want you. I'm taking the car to London and I shall be away about half-an-hour."

The chauffeur had disappeared when Delia Sennett came out.

"What a beautiful car!" she said. "Are you going to drive?"

Jimmy was on the point of answering when

an interruption occurred. He became suddenly conscious that there was a man standing in the drive. The red rear light illuminated for a second dimly the pattern of a trouser, and then from the gloom stepped a man.

"What do you want? Who are you?" asked Jimmy in surprise.

He had thought at first it was one of the servants of the house, but the light from the open door illuminated the stranger and at the sight of him Delia shrank back with a little cry. The man was young and poorly dressed. His puffed, unshaven face was set in a horrible grin, and Jimmy realized that he had been drinking.

"Hello, Delia darling!" chuckled the stranger. "Is this your new young man?"

She did not reply.

"What are you doing here?" asked Jimmy sternly.

"What am I doing? I'm looking after my girl, that's what I'm doing!" said the man, with a hiccough.

He lurched forward and put out an unsteady hand to grab the girl's arm, but Jimmy had made a quick and an accurate guess. This was the "mean man." He knew it instinctively and, gripping the stranger's arm, pushed him back.

"Let me go!" roared the man, and struggled to free himself.

There was a quick step in the passage, and old Joe Sennett came out into the night, peering out in his short-sighted way.

"I thought I heard you. What are you doing here, Tom Elmers?"

"I'm looking after Delia, that's what I'm doing. Let go of me, will you!" snarled Elmers, struggling to free himself from the grip on him arm.

"Who is this man, Mr. Sennett?"

"He's a worthless blackguard"; old Joe's voice trembled with anger. "He's the hound who's tried his best to ruin me! I'll deal with him!"

"Go back, Mr. Sennett," said Jimmy quietly. "Now, look here, Elmers, are you going to stop this nonsense? You've no right here and nobody wants you."

The girl had been a silent spectator, but now she came from the shadows.

"Mr. Elmers, I think you ought to go,"

she said. "You have done enough mischief already."

Suddenly, with a wrench, Tom Elmers broke away from Jimmy's restraining hand and, with a cry that was like a wild beast's, sprang at her. Before he could touch her, her father had leapt at him and flung him back against the car with such violence that he slipped down on the running board and sat gasping and breathless, staring up at the old man.

"Now get out," said Joe, "and don't let me ever see you near me or mine again, or I'll kill you!"

The shock seemed to have sobered the man, and he got up slowly and, with his head on his chest and his grimy hands thrust into his pockets, lurched into the darkness and out of sight.

Jimmy stood looking after him and wondered. That this was the girl's lover, or ever had been, was a preposterous suggestion and one which, for some reason, he resented.

"I think we'll go back and have some very strong coffee!" he said. "Miss Sennett, you look just as white as a sheet."

The incident had the effect of spoiling what he thought would be a pleasant tête-à-tête drive, for old Sennett changed his plans and decided that he would work no more that night, but the change of arrangement gave Jimmy an opportunity of learning the inward meaning of this extraordinary scene.

"Tom Elmers is a printer," said Joe when they were sitting back in the drawing-room. "I knew his father and took the boy into the office for the old man's sake. A very clever boy too, I'll say that for him; one of the cleverest mathematical compositors I know. There aren't many men who can 'set' problems. It requires a special training and a special knowledge of typography. We use an extraordinarily small 'face' of type for that work. Tom did this job very well. He used to come to our house fairly frequently. Then he started in to make love to Delia, and that's where his visits to our house ended. The boy was headstrong, wilful and vicious too, Mr. Blake," he added, looking Jimmy in the eye. "I didn't mind his threats, but when I found him monkeying with type in order to

get me into trouble, I discharged him from
the works. We print several important trade
newspapers, and one day, just as we were
going to press with one, I found that somebody had altered a paragraph so that it li-
belled the biggest advertiser in the paper! I
traced that paragraph back to Tom. He'd
handled it and he'd altered it after proofs
were passed—I gave him half an hour to get
out, but before he had gone, I know, as Mr.
Van Roon knows, that he must have spent
hours fooling with that type that was ready
to go to the foundry, resetting whole pages so
that the stuff read stupidly or scurrilously."

So that was the story, and Jimmy, for some
extraordinary reason, was relieved. He was
almost gay as he drove them on the way to
Ambrose Street, Camberwell, where they
lived; and the girl who sat by his side on the
journey was so far affected by his good spirits
that she was cheerful when he left her. Indeed, the only man who was not cheerful that
evening was Gerald Van Roon.

"I wish to heaven you hadn't abducted my
printer," he grumbled. "Those infernal

proofs have got to be gone through and Sennett had promised to stay until they were finished."

"What do you think of her?" asked Jimmy, and Gerald frowned.

"Think of her?" he repeated, puzzled. "Oh, you mean the girl?"

He let his queer head fall on one side and looked at Jimmy—he was a head taller than his cousin.

"Yes," he said thoughtfully, "a nice girl. I like her father very much."

"Her father!" snorted Jimmy and went to bed.

CHAPTER THREE

THE news took Jimmy's breath away.

"Me?" he said incredulously. "Are you sure, Jerry?"

Gerald had come into his bedroom with a bundle of letters in his hand and, sitting on the edge of the bed, had read one of these.

"But I don't know the Prime Minister," protested Jimmy. "The only Cabinet Minister I know is Stope-Kendrick, and he only slightly."

Gerald Van Roon looked uncomfortable.

"Well, the truth is, Jimmy," he said, "I asked for this invitation for you. I thought you would like it."

Jimmy laughed.

"You silly old owl," he said. "Of course I like it. I'll be charmed to lunch with the Prime Minister. I shall have something to boast about to my dissolute friends. What is the occasion?"

"He is giving a lunch to Maggerson. Maggerson and he are very great friends," explained Gerald, pacing up and down the room. "In fact, if John Chapelle hadn't gone in for politics he would have been a very passable scientist. That, I should imagine, is the bond between them. They were at school together, Chapelle and Maggerson; and I should imagine it is a sort of luncheon party in his honour. Maggerson has been nine months in the United States and in Mexico, and apparently he has been going in for biological study. He's an extraordinary all-round man. I've got a letter here from Schaffer. Do you read German?"

Jimmy shook his head.

"I would scorn—" he began, and then remembered that there was a little girl who did speak and read German, and therefore a knowledge of the German language was a very admirable accomplishment and not to be scoffed at. "Who is Schaffer?" he asked.

It was one of Gerald's sorrows that his cousin was profoundly ignorant on all matters pertaining to science, and he shook his head sadly.

"I suppose if you didn't know Maggerson you couldn't be expected to know Schaffer," he said patiently. "Schaffer, of Leipzig, is also, curiously enough, a great mathematician and a great biologist. He tells me in this letter that Maggerson is bringing from Mexico a new species of plant that he thinks solves one of the greatest problems which has ever confronted science, namely, the link between the organic and the inorganic."

"Oh yes," said Jimmy politely. "The missing link——"

Poor Gerald made a gesture of despair.

"I think there is nothing quite so pathetic as your attempt to be interested in intelligent subjects," he said. "Anyway, this plant has extraordinary properties, and he has brought a specimen for Schaffer, and old Schaffer is wild with excitement. What I can't understand is this," and he began reading rapidly in German.

"Splendid!" said Jimmy when he had finished. "What is it, a poem?"

To his surprise, Gerald seemed oblivious of the fact that his cousin did not understand the language. He walked to the window and looked out, shook his head, and turned to Jimmy.

"Extraordinary," he said, "amazing! And of course it is impossible!"

"Oh, yes!" agreed Jimmy. "Monstrous— I don't know what it is all about; I'm sure Schaffer is wrong."

"Anyway, Maggerson will be able to tell us."

"So long as he tells you and doesn't tell me," said Jimmy, flinging his legs out of bed. "And Jerry old boy, I've got to confess to you that I'm not interested in vegetables, even organic vegetables; and if I met Schaffer in the street I shouldn't know him, and if I knew him I shouldn't take my hat off to him, and I'm going to be bored to death, but I'll go to the lunch for the same reason as I would go to an execution or a wedding—for the thrill and sensation of it."

Jimmy could not remember having in his life entered that primmest of prim thorough-fares, Downing Street. The Premier's house impressed him as being ridiculously small and unimposing. His first impression of the interior was of the big cheerless hall, from whence led two passages. But the drawing-room was bright and homelike, and the Prime Minister, a thin æsthetic looking man with a mane of white hair, was not half so stiff and formal as Jimmy had expected.

"You're the unscientific James Blake, aren't you?" he said with a smile which put a hundred little creases into the corners of his eyes.

"I think I'm the most unscientific Blake that has ever happened, sir," said Jimmy.

"You seem to survive the atmosphere very well," smiled the Prime Minister. "How do you do, Van Roon? You have not seen Maggerson since he has been back?"

"No, sir," said Jerry. He nodded to a little man with a grey-lined face.

"Do you know everybody here?" asked the Prime Minister.

"No, sir," confessed Jimmy. "The fact is, I only know the fellows one meets at Ciro's and the Embassy."

"I don't think you'll meet anybody here who is a member," said the Prime Minister dryly. "You should know Lord Harry Weltman."

A tall, hard-looking man offered his hand, and Jimmy experienced a little shiver of excitement, for the Minister of Defence was not only the richest man in the country, but was reputedly the real master of the Cabinet.

"And Stope-Kendrick, I think you have met?"

The grave little man came forward, and Jimmy, remembering how they had met, grinned within himself. Stope-Kendrick was the Home Secretary, and Jimmy and he had met under exciting circumstances. Stope-Kendrick had driven his car from a concealed lane on to the main road, and Jimmy, careering along at fifty miles an hour on his Rolls, had neatly sliced a wheel from that gentleman's car. A large, genial cleric, with a stout rubicund face, proved to be the Lord Bishop of Fleet; and Jimmy guessed that the common interests these men had was the love of science and especially of mathematics.

Other men came in and were introduced. Jimmy met a famous banker and a famous sailor, who came over from the Admiralty in a hurry, with his neck-tie twisted under his ear—but Maggerson did not come. One o'clock struck, and ten minutes passed, and a quarter of an hour, and the Premier was getting restless.

"He's such an absent-minded beggar," Jimmy heard him say, "that he's as likely as not to turn into the British Museum and forget all about this lunch; or he may be wandering up and down Whitehall trying to locate Downing Street with a penny map. Maggerson would never ask a policeman— he's infinitely too clever to do a simple thing like that."

"Do you think, Prime Minister"—it was Stope-Kendrick who spoke—"that we ought to send a messenger to look for him?"

"I telephoned to his house half an hour ago, and his housekepeer said that she could get no reply from his rooms, so he had probably left."

"I'll go, sir," said Jimmy, feeling the least important member of the party. The fact that he had never met or seen Mr. Maggerson and was the last person in the world who should be sent in search of him seemed immaterial. Jimmy was being crushed under a sense of his unimportance and was glad to make his escape.

He went through the hall, down the steps, into Downing Street, and was half-way towards Whitehall, when a man turned the corner at a run and came pounding towards him. Jimmy instantly recognized him from the sketchy description which Van Roon had drawn on their way to town. He was a big, heavy, stout man, with long hair and a large womanish face; but what made Jimmy stop and stare open-mouthed at the apparition was his extraordinary attire. He was wearing an old brown velvet smoking coat, beneath which the jacket of his pyjamas showed. A pair of soiled grey trousers were buckled round the waist with a belt, and two gaudy carpet slippers completed his attire.

His hair was untidy, floating as he ran. The pyjama jacket was open at the neck and showed a woollen undershirt. He was breathing heavily, as though he had run a considerable distance; and the fact that he had attracted attention in the street was evidenced when in pursuit of him came two policemen and a small crowd of curious onlookers.

"Mr. Maggerson?" gasped Jimmy.

"Out of my way!" he roared and, thrusting the young man aside, dashed up the steps of 10 Downing Street, pushed the door open and flew across the hall with Jimmy in pursuit.

He evidently knew his way. He flung wide the door of the drawing-room and staggered in. A dead silence greeted his arrival. Jimmy, in the doorway, saw the Prime Minister's face lengthen in his astonishment, and then Maggerson spoke in a strangled voice.

"Chapelle!" he gasped. "My God! Chapelle, you must do something . . . something . . . you must stop The Terror! . . ."

And then he collapsed into the arms of Lord Harry Weltman.

CHAPTER FOUR

Jimmy drove Gerald Van Roon back to Blackheath, and neither of them spoke until they were in Jerry's study.

"I think we'll have some lunch," said Jimmy. "I've just realized that I've gone grubless since breakfast time."

"Do you think he was mad?" asked the troubled Gerald.

"Overworked," said Jimmy practically. "Let that be a warning to you, Jerry. Go to bed early and take plenty of exercise, and you'll live to a ripe old age. Sit up all night and spend the gorgeous days of summer in your evil-smelling laboratory, and I shall be pestered by reporters to give an account of your life and the cause of your unexpected demise."

"But Maggerson!" said Gerald wonderingly. "The greatest brain in the world!

Didn't you see him, Jimmy, whimpering like a little child? It was awful!"

"Did you see his slippers?" asked Jimmy. "They were awful, if you like! Oh, Mrs. Smith, get us some food, will you? We're starving. Anything, cold meat, cheese, pickles, but get it quick!"

When the housekeeper had fluttered out Jimmy found a cigar and lit it.

"My dear Gerald, there's nothing to get worried about," he said. "You friend Maggerson has been overdoing it. The same sort of thing happens to an athlete when he overtrains. He gets stale and flabby, and there's no reason why we shouldn't witness the same phenomenon where brains are concerned. Besides, if people go monkeying about with strange and mysterious plants——"

Gerald turned quickly.

"The plant?" he said softly. "I wonder . . . what did he mean by The Terror? It could have had nothing to do with the plant."

"Perhaps he's going to poison the country and dry up the earth," said Jimmy. "I read an awfully good story in one of the magazines about a thing like that happening. By Jove!

Suppose he's brought an uncanny vegetable —a sort of upas cabbage that throws a blight where its shadow falls!"

"Don't be ridiculous, Jimmy!" snapped Van Roon. "The legend of the upas tree is purely imaginary. The upas tree is the 'Antiaris toxicaria,' the gum of which——"

"I'll take your word for it," said Jimmy. "God bless you, Mrs. Smith; that beef looks fine! If there's one thing I enjoy more than another," Jimmy went on, as he placed a slice of red beef between two pieces of bread, "it is lunching with the Prime Minister of England. The least he could have done was to invite us in to dispose of the baked meats."

"How can you jest?" said Gerald Van Roon angrily. "Could one eat with the greatest mind in England dying in another room?"

"Not a bit of it," said Jimmy practically; "that wasn't death, it was hysteria. Perhaps old Maggerson has got himself tangled up in a love affair," he speculated outrageously as he poured forth the beer. "These old devils do that kind of thing. I saw the same symp-

toms with young Freddy Parker after he had
an interview with a chorus girl's mother. The
poor boy was positively wilting when he came
to John Stuart's flat, and we had to bring him
round with absinthe cocktails."

By the time he had finished talking Gerald
Van Roon had stalked majestically from the
room. Yet, for all his cheerfulness, Jimmy
had been impressed by what he had witnessed. He had helped to carry the uncon-
scious Maggerson into the Premier's study,
and, if the truth be told, his was the only head
cool enough to apply the exact treatment re-
quired. He had seen too many men stricken
with that super-hysteria which is called shell-
shock to have any doubt as to what was the
matter with Mr. Maggerson.

As to the cause he could only conjecture.
Being young and healthy and bubbling with
life, the loss of his lunch was almost as important a matter as the loss which the world
of science would sustain by the removal of
its brightest ornament. The only other worry
in his mind was whether this happening
would interfere with Jerry's proof correction,
for Mr. Sennett had made an appointment to

call that evening; and Jimmy, by judicious and artful questioning, had discovered that Delia Sennett was coming with him.

It was an unusual experience for him to look forward to meeting a woman, and yet, beyond any doubt, the most anticipated event of the day was her arrival. Mr. Sennett had evidently heard of the misfortune which had overtaken the great mathematician, and Jimmy was to discover that to this old printer too, Walter Maggerson was something of an idol. Before they had come Gerald had talked about postponing the consultation.

"I don't feel up to proof-reading to-night," he said. "This business has rather upset me."

"Rubbish!" said Jimmy loudly. "You ought to be ashamed of yourself, being affected by these purely—er—emotional happenings. I'm surprised at you, Jerry! Be scientific, old top!"

Gerald looked at him suspiciously.

"You haven't taken such a violent interest in science before," he said.

"I'm picking it up," replied Jimmy glibly. "I'm going to sit down to poor old Maggerson's calculus and read it from cover to cover."

Jerry laughed in spite of his trouble.

"You dear idiot," he said, "imagine reading a complicated time-table from cover to cover or a multiplication table, or the precepts of Confucius in the original language!"

"Anyway, Maggerson's better. I've telephoned an enquiry," said Jimmy. "He will be well enough to leave Downing Street by to-night."

"That's good news!" said Jerry gratefully. "What a thoughtful fellow you are!"

And so Sennett and his daughter came, and after Jimmy had hustled the old man into his cousin's library he took the girl round the garden and there learnt that the news of Mr. Maggerson's fit was common property.

"They live in a world of their own, these scientists," she said, "and I feel horribly out of it. Daddy is in that world, and your cousin; and I was afraid that you were too."

"Look upon me as Lucifer," said Jimmy. "I'm banished every time I try to get back into it."

She looked at him with a glint of amusement in her eyes.

"You're not—" she hesitated.

"Clever's the word you're trying to bowdlerize," said Jimmy.

"No, I'm not."

"I think these scientific gentlemen are most admirable, and I don't know how we should get on without them, because undoubtedly they are responsible for my car and the various aeroplanes which carried me through the war, and wireless telegraphy and all that sort of stuff; but I feel that I am doing science the best turn possible when I make the most use of its inventions."

He pulled out his watch.

"We've got an hour and a half before dinner," he said. "What do you say to a run through the garden of England to Sevenoaks and back?"

She hesitated.

"I'll ask Father," she said.

"What is the good of asking your father; he's walking hand in hand with Jerry through the Stone Age, and maybe you'll interrupt them just at the very minute when he's dis-

secting an ichthyosaurus or something equally
ghastly."

She nodded.

"All right, I'll go."

A quarter of an hour later they were
flying along a white ribbon of road between
hedges white with the frothy blossom of
hawthorn.

"How did your lesson go?" asked Jimmy
by way of making conversation.

"My lesson? Oh, the early morning one.
Did you remember?"

"Apparently," said Jimmy. "I think I'll
take lessons in German."

She shook her head smilingly.

"You're the kind of pupil that never makes
progress; and besides, I only teach women,"
she said.

"I know that," he lied; "but when I said
I'd take German I was thinking of Mrs.
Smith, my housekeeper. She's frightfully
keen on learning languages——"

But her laughter arrested his invention.

It was a quarter of an hour after dinner-
time when the car came rolling up the drive,
and he lifted her out, though she could have

dispensed with his assistance, being also young and active. He looked forward to having her for the rest of the evening, but at dinner Gerald told him that his work was finished; and, although he drove the old printer and his daughter back to Camberwell by the most circuitous route, he came back to the house to face a long and lonely evening at a ridiculously early hour.

CHAPTER FIVE

THERE had been a witness to the early departure of Delia and her father. Mr. Elmers had lain upon the grassy heath, immediately opposite to the Priory and in full view, wondering in his thick way just how he could satisfy his employer's remarkable curiosity. He had been given a commission which he had consciously failed, and indeed, recognizing its difficulty, had not attempted to execute. He was in the process of creating a well-tailored lie when Delia had gone home.

He waited until the dusk fell; then he rose and walked slowly towards his place of appointment, which was a little bar on the Charlton Road. The barmaid was on the point of telling him that the private saloon was not reserved for tramps, when the middle-aged gentleman, who had been sitting in the lounge the greater part of the evening, nodded to the new-comer; and, since this gentleman had been very generous in his expenditure, and had stricken awe into the two barmaids' souls by ordering an expensive wine, which had to be searched for in the cellar, she restrained the caustic remark which was on the tip of her tongue.

The generous guest was plump and jovial of countenance; he was well-dressed and well-jewelled; and the barmaid, a keen student of human affairs, had found it extremely difficult to "place" him. He was too soft a man for a bookmaker; too genial and abstemious for one of the local "gentry." He had a large and peculiar smile—one of those pouting smiles which gave the impression that he was amused at something quite different from the apparent cause of mirth.

"Ah, Tom, my boy," he said. He had a deep rich voice, had Mr. Palythorpe, a voice vibrant with good-nature and tolerance.

Tom Elmers blinked at the light, and rubbed his hand across his unshaven chin.

"I think I'll have a little spirits, Mr. Palythorpe," he said.

Mr. Palythorpe nodded to the barmaid and, sitting down in the Windsor chair he had occupied for two hours, flicked a speck of fluff from his well-creased trousers, and beamed benevolently at the youth as he tossed down his whisky.

"Have another and bring your glass over here."

Mr. Palythorpe tapped the table by his side.

"Well?" he asked, when Tom Elmers was seated. "Did you see your young lady as you expected?"

The attitude of Tom Elmers towards the man was that of a servant towards his master, struggling to assert himself against the suggestion of inferiority.

"Yes, I saw her," he said.

"Did you get a chance of speaking with her?"

"No, I didn't, Mr. Palythorpe," said the man apologetically. "There was another fellow there and old Joe—damn him."

"Ssh!" said Mr. Palythorpe reprovingly. "Is there any chance of your seeing her to-morrow?"

"A fine chance I shall have!" said Elmers discouragingly.

"Didn't you hear anything at the house?
Now, don't sulk!"

The last words were in quite a different
tone, and Mr. Elmers sat up.

"I listened," he said, "but I could only just
hear the voices and nothing more."

He had "listened" from a distance of a
hundred yards, but this Mr. Palythorpe did
not know.

"You don't know what happened to-day
then? What was she doing at Blackheath?
She was here yesterday."

Tom grinned.

"I think I know," he said with a little
chuckle. "Roon has had some trouble with
his proofs."

"Well?" said the other patiently.

"Old Sennett went down to see him and
took Miss Sennett. He always takes her
everywhere he goes nowadays, since the
rumpus I had with him."

Mr. Palythorpe was very patient indeed.
He leant back in his chair and surveyed the
other without favour, but his tone was gen-
iality itself.

"You told me this afternoon that you knew

one of the guests at the Prime Minister's luncheons, and you said that you were at his house last night. As you knew him——"

"By sight," protested Tom. "I had only seen him at the works."

"As you knew him I brought you down here to see him on some excuse or other," said Mr. Palythorpe insistently. "You also told me that Sennett—that was his name, wasn't it—and the young lady that you're fond of might visit that house and that it would be a much easier job for you to find out what happened at the Prime Minister's to-day. Instead of doing as I told you, which was to go into Greenwich or Blackheath village and get a shave, you went drinking."

"I've only had about two," protested Tom; "and besides, what could I find out?"

"You could discover what was the trouble at the luncheon party which the Prime Minister gave to Maggerson," said Mr. Palythorpe. His voice was low and very gentle, but as he leant forward to bring his face closer to the man's, it changed.

"Do you expect me to go on paying you wages for nothing?" he asked harshly. "Do you think I brought you here in order to provide you with drinks?"

"You know what my job is," said Tom sulkily. "I'm a compositor. You said you'd give me a job on your paper; you didn't say anything about wanting me to spy on customers."

Mr. Palythorpe got up, never taking his eyes from his companion.

"I don't think you and I understand one another," he said. "You had better come to my place, where I can talk."

At the foot of Blackheath Hill they found a taxi-cab. They drove to the West End of London. Mr. Palythorpe had a pleasant little flat near Half Moon Street, and although he was well aware that he was under police observation, that surveillance, which would have been fatal to any other man's peace of mind, did not disturb Mr. Palythorpe at all.

In his handsome little sitting-room Mr. Palythorpe grew frank and communicative.

The Right Honourable John Stamford Chapelle, Prime Minister of England, had many enemies, as was natural by reason of his position. But political enmity and private

hate have little in common. Mr. Palythorpe's
dislike of the great political leader was purely
personal. In the days when Chapelle had
been a private member and a prominent figure
in the courts, Mr. Palythorpe had discovered
some very damaging facts about his pretty
but somewhat flightly daughter, who was
married to a rich stockbroker, and Mr. Palythorpe had utilized his knowledge in the
usual way.

An anonymous letter had been sent to the
girl demanding payment for a certain indiscreet diary which had been filched by a servant under notice, and sent by the pilferer to
Mr. Palythorpe's office. The girl in her
alarm went to her father, and that was the
undoing of Palythrope, for Mr. Chapelle had
gone to work, despite his daughter's prayers
and entreaties, knowing, as he did, that a
blackmailer cannot be satisfied, and had scien-
tifically trapped Mr. Palythrope—not only
trapped him, but had conducted the case
against him with such skill that an unsym-
pathetic judge had sent this soft man to the
rigours and restrictions of Dartmoor Prison
for ten years, seven-and-a-half years of which

this genial gentleman, with the pouting smile, spent in planning revenge.

He had come out of gaol and had inaugurated a new paper, placing a figure-head in charge.

He did not tell Tom Elmers all this. All that he thought it was necessary to explain was, that he had a very excellent reason for desiring the Prime Minister's discomfort.

"You understand, Elmers, that I am giving you a good salary. When you couldn't get work anywhere else——"

"I'm the best mathematical compositor in the country," boasted Tom Elmers, his voice a little unsteady.

"Wonderful!" said the other sarcastically. "And you're the best judge of cheap whiskey in the country too."

"I didn't drink till she turned me down," said Tom surlily.

"She lost a good husband," said the sardonic Mr. Palythorpe. "Now, don't interrupt me. I am giving you a good salary, and you're not earning it. You told me you'd get me into touch with the Prime Minister's friends."

"So I can," said Tom Elmers arrogantly. "I tell you all these scientific fellows know him. Why, I've spent days with Mr. Maggerson, correcting his proofs; and I know Mr. Van Roon; and they're friends of Mr. Chapelle."

Palythorpe rubbed his chin.

"I suppose there's no chance of your getting back to Ponters'?" he asked. "If I had only known then what I know now I shouldn't have worried about trying to get official secrets."

"There's no ghost of a chance," said Tom savagely. "Old Joe hates me. He wouldn't have me within half a mile of him."

"What have you done?" asked the other curiously. "Did you steal something?"

"No," was the short reply.

"You must have done some fool thing. Were you drunk?"

"No, I tell you I didn't drink until she turned me down."

"Oh, the girl, of course!"

Mr. Palythorpe nodded.

"I suppose you started courting her, eh? But that wouldn't make him chuck you out of

the office," he said, eyeing the other keenly.
"What was the reason?"

"Oh, nothing!" replied Tom, and then:
"What do you want to find out about Mr.
Chapelle?" he asked suddenly.

Palythorpe did not immediately reply.
When he did, it was parabolically.

"Every man has some secret in his life
which he doesn't want made public. The best
and the greatest of them have that, Elmers.
I haven't been in this game for years without
knowing that the perfect man doesn't exist.
Why, there are twenty people in London, men
who hold big positions, whom I could ruin if
I took the risk! But I don't want to take the
risk; there's nothing to it. But give me something about Chapelle, something that's going
to hurt him like hell, and I'll print it, if I
serve twenty years for the job!"

"I see, you want some scandal," said Tom.

"I not only want scandal, but I think I've
got it. There was something queer happened
in Downing Street to-day."

Palythorpe was talking as much to himself
as to his companion.

"I have a housemaid inside 10 Downing

Street who keeps me well informed of what happens," he said with a certain amount of pride. "What do you think of that? And something *has* happened which the Prime Minister is trying to hush; and if he wants to hush it up, that's good enough for me to make it as public as possible. That's all. We've got to find what it was."

"It seems easy," said Tom—it was the first hint he had given that he possessed a sense of humour.

CHAPTER SIX

USUALLY Jimmy Blake found no difficulty in amusing himself between dinner and bedtime. If he was not engaged in town, there was generally a novel to be got through, or he would potter about in the garage with the chauffeurs, or he would take to pieces his motor-bicycle (a weakness of his), but tonight time dragged. Even "demon patience" had no attraction, and he wandered disconsolately into Jerry's study and stood watching him enviously, for it was Gerald Van Roon's complaint that there were only twenty-four hours in the day and that he had to waste seven of these in sleep.

"What are you doing, Jerry?" he asked complainingly.

"I'm doing an article for the *Scientific Englishman*," said Gerald, looking up, by no means pleased at the interruption.

"What about?" asked Jimmy, seating himself uninvited and then proceeding to light a cigarette.

Gerald Van Roon pushed his chair back from the table with an air of resignation.

"It is in relation to a controversy which has recently arisen in scientific circles as to whether the scientist should take the public into his confidence in moments of national emergency."

"What do you think?"

"I believe that the public should know," said Gerald. "The controversy arose as to the scare of last spring that the wheat and root harvest would fail owing to the presence of some micro-organism which had made a mysterious appearance. It looked as though the world was going to be starved of bread and roots. The thing was kept dark and happily the danger did not materialize, but I say that the public should have been told."

"What does it matter whether they should have been told or shouldn't have been told? It's all over now," said Jimmy lazily. "What a queer old fish you are, Jerry! Put down your pen and come out and be human. I'm bored stiff and I've half a mind to go up to London and see a revue. It doesn't start until nine o'clock, and we should only miss half an hour of it."

Gerald shook his head.

"Come along," urged his cousin. "You needn't dress."

"I'm not interested in revues or theatres, and nobody knows that better than you, Jimmy," said the other irritably. "Besides, I must finish this article to-night."

Jimmy rose with a sigh and loafed back to his own den. He tried to read, but his mind was not upon the page. The phrase "falling in love" is more or less a figure of speech to denote an unusual attraction and interest in a person of the opposite sex, plus an extraordinary sense of loss when he or she has temporarily gone out of one's life. It is this sense of missing which, stimulating and magnifying the pleasure of reunion, gives a false value to what is no more than a passing liking. Delia, from the first moment he saw her, was attractive to him. There was something about her which was ineffably sweet and feminine. She was serene without being complacent; efficient, but not terrifyingly so.

There was not a scrap of affectation in her make-up—Jimmy told her himself that she was the most natural creature he had ever met. He wondered how she spent her evenings. Did she ever go to theatres or dinners? He had not even suggested he should meet her. He could do nothing surreptitious or furtive, and he was conscious that anything in the nature of a clandestine meeting would be repugnant to her as it was to him.

She lived in a tiny house which was one of fifty other tiny houses in a drab suburban street. She had no mother, she had told him. She and her father lived alone, a woman coming in in the daytime to do the housework. What a life for a girl . . . a girl like Delia! He strolled restlessly into the drawing-room and sat down opposite to the chair from which, an hour before, she had rested her deep blue eyes on his as he recounted an air adventure which had all but ended in his finish. He could picture her every movement, the quick movement of her pink hands, the sudden uplift of her eyebrows, the softening of her look when he spoke of his friend who had been shot down and had died in Jimmy's arms.

He got up quickly and, cursing himself for an idiot, went back to his study.

This time he did make some attempt to write letters, and working up an interest in the subject he was fully occupied when the door of the study opened and Gerald appeared.

At the sight of him Jimmy stared.

"Where the dickens are you going?" he asked, for Gerald was dressed and was wearing a light raincoat. What interested the other more than his attire was the seriousness of his cousin's face.

"I've got to go out, Jimmy," said Van Roon. "I don't know how long I shall be away, but please don't wait up for me; I have a key."

"Where are you going?"

Gerald shook his head.

"I'm afraid I can't tell you. I've been asked to keep the matter confidential, and I'm afraid I must keep my movements a secret."

"Has it anything to do with Maggerson?"
Gerald hesitated.

"I can't even tell you that," he said briefly.
"Don't ask me, old boy, and don't sit up for
me! I can tell you this, that I haven't the
slightest idea what the business is all about."

"It sounds like a conspiracy to me," smiled
Jimmy. "Well, so long. Keep away from
the drink!"

He sat a little longer at his desk, but he
did not work. Presently he rose and, going
in search of his butler, found him locking up.

"Who was it came for Mr. Van Roon?"
asked Jimmy.

"I don't know, sir. To tell you the truth,
Mr. Blake, I was sitting under the porch
having a quiet pipe before I went to bed, a
habit of mine, sir, for thirty years, as you
well know."

"Don't tell me the story of your life,
Stephens," said Jimmy testily. "Who came
for Mr. Van Roon?"

"Well, sir, I saw two people coming up the
drive. They must have seen the glow of
my pipe, because they stopped; and then one
of them came on.

" 'Is this Mr. Van Roon's house?' this gentleman asked, and he was a gentleman by his tone.

" 'Begging your pardon, sir, this is Mr. Blake's house, but Mr. Van Roon lives here,' says I."

Jimmy chuckled at the distinction.

" 'I've a letter for him which is very urgent,' said the gentleman, and all the time he kept about half a dozen paces from me. 'Will you come and get it?'

"I thought it was very strange, his not coming up to the front door, but I went down the drive and took it from his hand."

"Did you recognize him?" asked Jimmy.

The butler shook his head.

"No, sir, he had his coat collar turned up. It's raining, I suppose you know, and I didn't catch sight of so much as the tip of his nose. I took the letter in to Mr. Van Roon, and he opened it and read it and he seemed a bit surprised. That is all I know, sir."

"Did you let Mr. Van Roon out?"

"No, sir, he let himself out. I've got an idea that the gentlemen were waiting for him."

"That's queer," said Jimmy. "All right, Stephens, lock up. Good night."

And Jimmy went back to his study, which was a big room on the ground floor communicating by French windows to the lawn and the tennis court.

He looked at his watch. It was a quarter to twelve. His curiosity was piqued. Who on earth were these mysterious individuals with their "coat collars turned up" and presumably their hats pulled over their eyes like melodramatic plotters? That wasn't Gerald Van Roon's line at all. He dealt in simple things, or simple they were to him, like bugs and reaction tests and uninteresting bits of stone, and masses of calculations. There was no romance in his soul, or woman in his life; and people did not call him out at midnight to discuss the atomic theory or the differential calculus.

Jimmy found a pack of cards and spent an unprofitable hour playing patience. At one o'clock he went to the front door, opened it and looked out. A thin drizzle of rain was falling, but behind the clouds was a hint of a moon. Save for the drip, drip of rain, there was no sound. He thought he had heard the wheels of a taxi-cab, but it was on the other side of the Heath, on the road running parallel with the boundary wall of Greenwich Park.

He threw his cigarette away and went back to his study again. Two o'clock came, but there was no sign of Gerald. For some extraordinary reason his absence was getting on Jimmy's nerves. It was not an unusual thing for one or the other to be out at night, and to worry was stark lunacy. Perhaps it was because the method of Jerry's going had been so odd that Jimmy's nerves were on edge. He shuffled his cards and then began to deal "sevens."

He stopped suddenly, a card in his hand, and listened. He had heard something, and now he heard it again, a "tap, tap" on the study window. The sound was muffled by the curtains and the shutters which covered the French casement, but unmistakably it came from the study window. Perhaps Jerry had forgotten his key after all. He got up quickly, went out into the hall and opened the door.

"Is that you, Jerry?" he asked.

He saw a slight figure coming towards him, the figure of a woman.

"Who is that?" he asked.

"It is Delia Sennett," said a soft voice, and Jimmy's jaw dropped.

"Delia!" he said, hardly believing his ears. "Good heavens! Whatever are you doing out at this time of night? Come in!"

She was clad in a long mackintosh shiningly wet, and he helped her off with it. There was only a momentary glint of amusement in her eyes as she looked up to him, and he saw that she was deeply troubled.

"Come into the study," he said. "This is the most extraordinary happening! Where is your father?"

"He left me just as your door opened," she said.

Jimmy could only sit and stare at her when she told her story.

"About an hour ago, perhaps a little more, after Daddy and I had gone to bed," she said, "somebody knocked at the door, and Father went down and answered it. I thought at first it was Tom Elmers and I was frightened, because Tom has made threats against

Father which he may, in his madness, carry out. Daddy was a long time gone, and I got out of bed, put on my dressing-gown and went half-way down the stairs, when he heard me, and ordered me to stay where I was. Then he came up and told me that he'd been called out on very important business. I think I should have agreed to staying in the house alone, but he wouldn't hear of it. He went downstairs again, and I heard him talking to somebody at the door; who it was, he would not say; and then he came back.

" 'Delia,' he said, 'I'll take you to Mr. Van Roon's house and leave you there. Perhaps the housekeeper will look after you. I shall be out all night.' It had been raining when I went to bed and I did not want to go out, but he insisted. He said whatever happened he couldn't leave me in the house alone. That was nothing new," she explained with a little nod. "Ever since—Mr. Elmers was so un-pleasant, Father has refused night duty. So I dressed, came down and found a taxi-cab waiting. The man who came for Father had disappeared. We drove till we came to the end of the Heath—this Blackheath—and then we got down. I thought I saw a car waiting at the side of the road and I have an idea that the car had come on before us. From there we walked to the Priory, and that is all I know."

"You don't know where your father's gone?"

"I haven't the slightest idea," said the girl.

"Has he gone back to London?"

"He may have done"; she shook her head in a hopeless fashion, and then they both laughed.

"Jerry isn't in yet; I'm expecting him every minute. He's had a mysterious summons too."

Before Jimmy went upstairs to rouse Mrs. Smith he told her what had happened earlier in the evening. Mrs. Smith, like the good old soul she was, came bustling down in her preposterous dressing-gown and fussed around Delia like an old hen round a derelict chick, and in half an hour they had sent their charge off to bed and Jimmy continued his vigil.

Four o'clock came and brought no word from Jerry. Dawn had broken when Jimmy stepped again into the garden. The rain had ceased, the clouds were dispersing, and there was a promise of a fine day. He walked down the drive to the road and stood smoking. He looked along the road and across the shadowy Heath. The only sign of life, was the movement of a big white motor-car which was coming from the direction of Woolwich on the park side of the Heath. Instead of passing along towards the Deptford road, it stopped, turned and then remained stationary.

Jimmy was interested, and wondered what was the meaning of the manœuvre. Then he saw a cyclist skimming across the Heath path and only knew it was a cyclist by the rapidity with which it moved. Near at hand it proved to be a policeman. Jimmy shouted a "Good morning," and the policeman stopped and jumped down.

"I suppose you haven't anybody missing from this house, sir?" he asked.

"No," said Jimmy, and then remembering with a start. "My cousin hasn't come home yet, but I am expecting him any moment."

"Oh, not a lady?" said the policeman, turning to mount.

"No, a gentleman; Mr. Van Roon."

The policeman turned.

"What sort of a man was he in appearance, sir?"

"He is rather tall," said Jimmy.

"How was he dressed?" asked the policeman quickly.

"In a black coat and vest and grey trousers," said Jimmy in alarm. "Why, what has happened?"

"A gentleman has been killed on the Heath —if he's not dead now, he will be soon. They're just taking him to the Herbert Hospital. He wore grey trousers and a black coat. Did your cousin wear horn-rimmed spectacles?"

Jimmy's heart sank.

"Yes," he said huskily.

"Well, that's the man," said the policeman. "He's been shot to pieces, and I doubt if he'll live till he gets to the hospital."

"Good God!" gasped Jimmy and went white. "Just come in here, Constable."

Quickly he led the way into the house, and the policeman followed. Jimmy took up a photograph of Gerald from his study table and handed it to the constable. The man nodded.

"Yes, sir, that's the gentleman," he said quietly.

Jimmy bit his lip. Gerald! A man without an enemy in the world. It seemed incredible!

"Do you mind going up to the second floor, knocking on every door and telling the servants what has happened?" he said. "I'll get my car out of the garage. The Herbert?" he said. "That's the military hospital?"

"Yes, sir. We had to get a military ambulance for him."

Jimmy ran to the garage and soon the big Rolls was flying across the Heath. By this time the ambulance had disappeared. Later he saw it waiting empty outside the principal entrance of Herbert Hospital. In the entrance hall of the building were two policemen. They were talking to a military doctor and turned at Jimmy's appearance.

"You think you know him, sir, do you?"

"I'm afraid I do," said Jimmy breathlessly. "Is he still living?"

The Doctor nodded.

"That is as much as I can say," he said. "He is in the surgery. I have left him on the stretcher—we dare not move him."

Jimmy followed the officer through a door and there, lying on the floor on the brown canvas stretcher, his face white and his lips queerly blue, was Gerald Van Roon!

Jimmy choked a sob and knelt down by the side of the dying man. Gerald must have sensed the nearness of his friend, for he opened his eyes and his lips twisted in a little smile. He tried to speak, and Jimmy bent his head down until his ear was against the cold lips.

". . . I was a fool. . . . I didn't realize . . . Schaffer's letter . . . forgot all about it . . . show it to them, Jimmy. . . ."

And here his voice ceased suddenly.

Gerald Van Roon was dead.

CHAPTER SEVEN

JIMMY drove back to the house, his heart like lead. He went straight to his study, locked the door and, throwing himself down on the sofa, wept as he had never thought it possible for a grown man to weep. He had loved Jerry. They had been companions since they were boys. They understood one another, and Jimmy's acute sense of loss shocked and desolated him.

Presently he got up with an aching head and, going to his room, took a cold shower. Moses brought him a cup of strong tea and made no comment upon his appearance. Jimmy now realized that as the household knew of the tragedy it would be difficult to keep the news from the girl. On the whole, after consideration, he thought she had better know. It would be hardly possible to keep such a secret. He was at breakfast when she came down, and as she passed him to her place, she laid her hand for a moment on his shoulder and there was something so eloquent in that expression of sympathy that Jimmy nearly broke down again.

"I've been blubbing like a kid all the morning. What do you think of that for a grown man?" he asked with self-contempt.

"I should have expected you to," she said quietly, and then he remembered her own little worry.

"Your father hasn't returned yet?"

"No, but I have had a note from him. It came down from London by messenger. He has been at work at his office most of the night and he said he would fetch me this evening."

"He couldn't stay here, I suppose?" asked Jimmy. "I shall hate being alone. It's rather far from his office, but he could go up by car every morning and we could fetch him every night."

She was silent, knowing that it was a woman's presence he needed, and that woman, she.

"I'll ask him when he comes to-night," she said.

"It will be rather gloomy for you," said

Jimmy with sudden contrition, but she smiled.

A little after breakfast a detective called at the house, and then Jimmy learnt the details of the tragedy, which were very few. A constable on patrol duty had seen a man lying on the Heath in the early light of dawn, and going towards him was horrified to discover that he was bleeding from four or five wounds. He had been shot at close range with an automatic pistol, in the hands of somebody who was not used to the employment of fire-arms, said the detective, and gave reasons for his conclusion. The body had been found at the point where Blake had seen the ambulance, about fifty yards from the postern gate of the Warden's Lodge.

It was when he accompanied the detective to Gerald's study that he realized how useful the girl might be if she could give the time to the service. The desk and innumerable pigeon-holes were littered with sheets and scraps of closely-written memoranda, and when these came to be examined, Jimmy found that they were written in Dutch. There was, too, a great deal of correspondence in French and German, for poor old

Gerald had been in touch with the leading scientists of both countries.

Schaffer's letter! Jimmy remembered the last words of the dying man, which he had almost believed were spoken in delirium.

"I was a fool. . . . I didn't realize . . . Schaffer's letter!"

He remembered the letter from Schaffer. Gerald had sat on the edge of the bed and read voluble extracts in German which meant nothing to Jimmy. After the detective had left, he began a search of the desk. There were several letters in German. Some were signed with names, some with initials. Jimmy went in search of the girl and found her in his study. He told her what had happened at the hospital.

"I thought the poor old chap wasn't right in his head and I didn't attach much importance to what he said; but he distinctly said, 'Schaffer's letter,' and he asked me to show it to them—who 'them' are—heaven knows!"

"It was in German, you say?" she said as she accompanied him back to Gerald's room.

He sat watching her as she went quickly and systematically through the papers which covered the big writing-table. At the end of her search she shook her head.

"There are several letters from Germans here," she said, "but there is nothing from Schaffer. Do you remember where he lived?"

"In Leipzig, I think."

"There is only one letter from Leipzig and that is from a Dr. Bohn. Perhaps it is in his room."

Jimmy went up to his cousin's room and conducted a careful search, but there was no sign of correspondence. In the fireplace were ashes, and these Jimmy brought to the light. The writing was still visible, a queer black glaze upon a duller black; and he carried the portions of the ashes he could retrieve to the study.

"This is from Mr. Schaffer"; she pointed to a scrawl at the end of the burnt paper. "But it's almost impossible to read, except this little bit."

She carried the shovel on which he had laid the ashes to the big window of the study.

"I can read something. 'I cannot believe that the Herr Maggerson could have made so—' and that is all," she said disappointedly. "I wish I could have read more of it for you."

"Poor old Jerry must have burnt it," said Jimmy, "and then forgot he burnt it! I wonder what it was all about?"

Delia had an appointment in London that morning, but resolutely refused to accept the use of the car.

"I can go by train," she said; "and I can come back to-night, can't I?"

"You've got to come back," he said almost brusquely. "I want you to tackle this correspondence of Jerry's, and give me a translation of all the foreign letters. Will you accept that as a commission? And as to your staying here, Delia, well, I'll see your father about it."

He walked with her to the station and returned, but not to the house. He made his way towards the place where the body had been found, and he had no difficulty in locating the exact spot, for two detectives were taking measurements under the eyes of a small crowd.

The afternoon papers made a feature of the murder. Gerald Van Roon had a European reputation; the terrible nature of his end, the mystery which surrounded it, and the absence of all clues gave the case an additional importance.

Reporters came to the Priory (he remembered with a pang how he had jestingly predicted their advent), but Jimmy, acting on the advice of the police, said nothing about the curious circumstances which attended Gerald's going out on the previous night. When he had got rid of them he went to his room to think. He connected the summon to Gerald with the equally inexplicable summon to Joe Sennett.

When Sennett came that evening, preceding his daughter by half an hour, he had little or nothing to tell.

"The only thing I can tell you is this, Mr. Blake," he said. "I was called out on Government service. We print all the confidential circulars for the Ministries; and it was not unusual, especially during the war, for me to be turned out of bed in the early hours to set up and 'pull'—that is to say, print with a hand-press—secret documents."

"Do you set them up yourself?"

"Either myself or one other man, invariably," said the printer.

"What were those instructions?" Jimmy knew it was a foolish question before he had finished the sentence.

"Well, I can hardly disclose that," smiled the other, "but I'll tell you this much, Mr. Blake, that they were for the military and seemed to me to be sufficiently important to justify arousing an elderly and respectable printer from his bed."

"Where did you go for your instructions?" persisted Jimmy, and Joe Sennett's face became blank.

"That is another of the questions I can't answer, Mr. Blake. I'm very sorry. I can only tell you that I had to go to a certain house, interview a member of the Government, who gave me a certain document, written by his own hand; and that I prepared three hundred copies by this morning—as Mr. Van Roon will tell you——"

Jimmy's eyes opened wide.

"Mr. Van Roon?" he said incredulously.

"Haven't you heard? Haven't you seen the papers?"

"No, sir," said the startled old man. "Has anything happened?"

"Mr. Van Roon was murdered in the early hours of this morning, and his body was found near the Warden's Lodge," said Jimmy slowly.

The effect upon Joe Sennett was remarkable. He turned white and fell back against the panelled wall of the study.

"Near the Warden's House?" he said in a hollow voice. "Dead? Murdered? Impossible! He was alive at three o'clock. I saw him!"

Jimmy uttered a cry.

"You saw him at three! Where?" he demanded, but Joe's lips were set.

"That I cannot tell you, sir," he said; "but when I saw him he was in good company."

There was a silence.

"Mr. Sennett, you will have to tell the police that," said Jimmy quietly, and the old man nodded. "But can't you tell me some more?"

"I'm afraid I can't, sir," said Joe in a low voice. "I was fond of Mr. Van Roon and I'd do anything in the world to bring his murderers to justice, but I saw him in circumstances where my lips are sealed."

Jimmy nodded.

"I won't worry you any more about it," he said sadly; "if you promise to see the police and tell them all you know, I must be satisfied."

And then, by way of turning the conversation, Jimmy made his suggestion that Sennett and his daughter should stay at the house. To his surprise, Joe accepted almost without hesitation.

"If you don't mind putting us up, and I shan't be in your way, I shall be glad, sir; and I shall be more glad for Delia's sake too. If I'm liable to be called out in the middle of the night, and I think that this won't be the only time I shall be away from home, I should be worried about the girl."

She came in soon after and learnt of his decision. Jimmy, watching her to see whether she was pleased or perturbed, failed to detect sign of either feeling. She went to bed early, and he, at a loose end and beginning to feel the reaction of the day, dozed in his chair. The night was a little chilly, and the fire had gone out when he woke with a shiver. It was twelve o'clock, twenty-four hours from the time Gerald Van Roon had left the house, never to return.

Jimmy was wide awake now and less inclined for bed than ever. He found Stephens the butler smoking his pipe in the porch, a night-cap pipe which, as he had truly said, was the habit of half a life-time.

"I'm going for a stroll across the Heath," said Jimmy shortly. "Wait up till I come back."

The man was concerned.

"Do you think it wise to go out at night, sir?"

"Don't be silly, Stephens," snapped Jimmy. "Bring me a walking stick."

It had clouded up again and the night was dark. Something led him irresistibly to the spot where Gerald had been found. In the darkness it was difficult to locate the exact position, and he stood as near as he could guess and tried to reconstruct the crime. He was fifty yards from the roadway, a little more than that distance from the dark wall which hid the Warden's Lodge. The detective had told him casually in conversation that morning that the Warden's Lodge was untenanted and had been so for fifteen years.

Jimmy heard the whirr of an engine; saw a pair of motor-car lights coming along the Park road. It stopped a quarter of a mile from him and he heard the slam of a door. Then the car turned about and went back the way it had come. Who had alighted so far from a house? he wondered. He heard a brisk foot-step coming along the road, and it occurred to him that the pedestrian, whoever he might be, would, if he had some knowledge of the tragedy that had occurred the night before, be considerably alarmed to see a figure standing in the place where the body was found. It was out of consideration for the walker's feelings rather than for any other reason that he sat down on the grass.

Nearer came the man and when opposite Jimmy stopped and turned—towards the postern door of the Warden's Lodge!

Jimmy heard a key grate in the lock, the snap of the wards, and the door opened and closed softly. One of the Park wardens, he told himself, but a park-keeper would not come in a car, nor dismiss it a quarter of a mile from his destination.

Jimmy waited. Again came the drone of wheels, this time it was unmistakably a taxi. This vehicle also stopped, but a little farther away than had the first car, and again Jimmy heard the bang of a door and saw the taxi turn and its red tail-lights vanishing over the hill.

The second man walked much slower than the first, and he carried a walking stick. In the still night Jimmy heard the tap of it as he came nearer. Also he walked more in the shadow of the wall, and the watcher did not see him until he was against the postern door. Again a key was inserted, again came the snap of the lock. Almost on the heels of the second man came a third. This time the car stopped at about the same place as the first had come to a standstill and then continued on its way, flashing past Jimmy in the direction of Woolwich.

Whether it was empty or not he could not see, but after a while he heard the third man's feet on the road, and the same things occurred as before. He also passed through the

postern gate, locking the door behind him.
A fourth man arrived on a cycle. Jimmy saw
the light far away and then it appeared to be
suddenly extinguished. It looked as though
the man had stopped for the purpose of blow-
ing it out. At any rate, the machine came
on noiselessly and invisibly, and the first intimation Jimmy received of the stranger's arrival was when he jumped from the bicycle
and trundled it across the path to the gate.
He, too, passed through and was the last arrival Jimmy saw, although he waited until
the church clocks were striking two.

He walked across to the Priory with his
head swimming. Stephens was waiting for
him at the entrance of the drive.

"Thank God you're back, sir," he said
shakily. "I've been so worried about you,
Mr. Blake!"

"Make me some coffee or tea or something," said Jimmy; but when Stephens came
back with a steaming cup, he found Jimmy
curled up on the sofa fast asleep, and, finding
he could not rouse his master, loosened his
collar, took off his boots and, covering him
with a rug, left him; in return for which

service he was heartily cursed the next morning by a stiff and weary Jimmy, since, when he woke up, Delia had gone to town.

After he had bathed and changed he went across the Heath to make a closer inspection of the Warden's Lodge.

The Warden's Lodge stood back from the road and all view of the house was entirely obstructed by a wall, a continuation of the main wall of Greenwich Park. Entrance to the house and its grounds was obtained through a heavy postern gate painted sage green. The Lodge was Government property and in earlier days had housed a royal "ranger," but was now, apparently, empty. Crossing the roadway after inspecting the gate, Jimmy had to walk a considerable distance over the Heath before he could so much as catch a glimpse of the Lodge proper, and then the only view presented was a corner of a parapetted and presumably flat roof and a portion of a chimney. The rest was hidden behind four leafy chestnut trees.

On the top of the wall were *chevaux de frise* of steel spikes, mounted on a rod which probably revolved at a touch. The other entrance to the Lodge was from Greenwich Park, upon which its grounds impinged, and this could only be reached through the Park gates, a few hundred yards further along.

Jimmy was baffled. In the first place the Lodge was royal property and, although neglected and untenanted, would be all the time under the observation of the park-keepers and officials. Obviously, it could not be in the occupation of unauthorized persons for any length of time. And yet it was being used almost openly by a mysterious party of men, each of whom possessed a key which opened the green gate.

Stephens had gone to Woolwich, to the hospital, to make the final arrangements for Gerald's funeral; and this last ordeal and service Jimmy rendered to his cousin that afternoon. He and a dozen men, most of whom were elderly professors, were the chief mourners at that melancholy function. Maggerson, he did not expect; nor was there any message of any kind from him or from the Prime Minister.

Jimmy got back to the house about five o'clock, very sick at heart, and found that

Delia had not returned. There was an evening paper lying on his study table and, opening it, he looked for news about the murder. There was a column of matter, but nothing that he did not already know. A tramp had been arrested at Charlton, but had accounted for his movements on the night of the outrage.

What seemed strange to Jimmy was the fact that the police had not been again to the house. He had written a note making reference to Schaffer's letter and his cousin's last words; and he had anticipated the early arrival of the police officers, but they seemed satisfied with the possibility he had suggested, that Gerald may have been delirious at the moment he spoke. The house was strangely empty and Jimmy was as unhappy as he could be. He loafed upstairs to his room and then remembered that Gerald had had a little workroom, a tiny observatory he had built at a time when he was preparing a series of lectures on the moon's rotation.

The Priory had a flat roof, and upon this, on Gerald's instructions, there had been built a small hut of galvanized iron. It was empty, with the exception of a table, a chair, three or four sheets of dusty paper, and a large telescope on a tripod, which poor Jerry had used for his lunar observations.

"By Jove!" said Jimmy.

It was not any discovery he had made in the hut which had startled him to this exclamation, but the fact that from one of the three windows of the hut he had a fairly clear view of a part of the Warden's Lodge. From here, the view dodged two trees and showed at least three windows and a length of parapet of this mysterious lodge. He decided to go down for his glasses and then his eyes lit on the telescope. He dragged the tripod forward and, sitting down at the eye-piece, he focussed the instrument upon the house. Such was its high magnification that it brought the Lodge so close that Jimmy had the illusion that by putting out his hand he could touch the windows.

He got up and cleaned the lenses, which were dusty; then came back and carefully scrutinized as much of the building as was visible. One of the windows was open at the top. He wished it were open at the bottom, for in the present state of the light he could not see through the reflecting surfaces of the glass.

He was looking at the window, when he saw something that made him jump. Through the silvery reflection loomed a face. At first it was blurred and indistinct, but at it approached the glass every line and curve of the face was visible. It was the face of Maggerson, the mathematician! He was haggard, untidy; his hair was all awry and a stray lock fell over his forehead, giving him a comically dissolute appearance—but it was Maggerson —staring almost into Jimmy's eyes. Only for a second did it show, and then it vanished as suddenly as it had appeared.

CHAPTER EIGHT

JIMMY BLAKE had known sympathy in his life, but he had never appreciated or experienced the beautiful quality of tenderness which a woman can give to the sorely hurt. Delia's understanding was shown in a score of ways, even her silences had a soothing value. She had the gift of changing the direction of a conversation, so that it was turned before the participants realized in what unhappy direction the talk was heading. She was cheerful in her sweet, quizzical way; and Jimmy had found himself challenged to flippant retort—on the day he had buried Gerald Van Roon! She could give the whole of one day that week, she told him, to the examination of Gerald's papers.

"Do you remember what was in the Schaffer letter? You said that poor Mr. Van Roon had read a portion of it to you."

"The portion he read was in German.

Poor old boy, he was very absent-minded—
he even forgot that he had burnt it!" smiled
Jimmy. "But he did tell me that Schaffer
said something about Maggerson bringing
back a queer plant from New Mexico—or
Mexico—I'm not sure which."

"What kind of plant?"

"It was a plant which established the connection between something or other," said
Jimmy vaguely. "Oh yes, I remember; between the organic and the inorganic."

"That is rather important, isn't it?" she
said, interested. "Science has never discovered the link——"

"That's it! I joked the old fellow about
it. I called it the 'missing link,' and he was
absolutely sick with me!"

She bit her lip thoughtfully.

"I wonder if that had anything to do with
it," she said, speaking to herself.

"To do with Jerry's murder," asked
Jimmy, astonished. "What on earth could
that have to do with it?"

"He spoke about Schaffer's letter. I'm
sure he knew what he was saying," said the
girl. "He recognized you and remembered

that he had shown you the letter in the morning."

"That is true," said Jimmy, impressed.

"Why don't you see Mr. Maggerson and ask him?" she suggested.

It was on the tip of his tongue to tell her that he had seen Maggerson less than two hours before, but he stopped himself. He wanted to know something more about the Warden's Lodge and he had already made up his mind to undertake a second vigil that night. But as to this he had decided that it would be better if he took nobody into his confidence, not even Delia. After she had gone to bed, he strolled out without telling Stephens where he was going, and took up his position near to the spot he had occupied the night before.

This time he had brought a light waterproof sheet, which he laid on the ground, for the grass had been wet the previous night. It was ten minutes after twelve when the first car appeared, and the happenings of the previous night were repeated almost exactly. One man came after another, and Jimmy, lying full-length on the ground, focussed the night-glasses he had brought with him upon each in turn, without, however, discovering their identity. If only the moon would show! But the moon was represented in the sky by a pale patch of light behind the low-hanging clouds.

At two o'clock he returned to the Priory, determined that the next night he would force a recognition. The plan that he roughly formed was this: as soon as a car appeared and he know that the passenger was on his way to the Lodge, he would walk to meet him and, on some excuse or other, turn the beam of a hand lamp on his face. Know them he would, for it was impossible to avoid associating this unknown four with Van Roon's death.

But why had Jerry said nothing which would incriminate them? All his thoughts had been of Schaffer's letter. It was queer. As he was going to bed that night he had another idea, and the next morning drove the girl up to London and, dropping her in the City, went on to Whitehall.

Stope-Kendrick was not exactly a friend of his, but they had met at the Prime Min-

ister's house and he did not think that the
Home Secretary would refuse to see him.
That worthy gentleman, however, had not
arrived when Jimmy called, nor was he in
his office until after mid-day, when Jimmy
presented his card for the third time and was
ushered into a great and gloomy room where
the little man sat behind a table which further
dwarfed his stature.

He was looking very ill. There were deep
shadows under his eyes and his face was a
pasty white. His manner, however, was vig-
orous and almost cheerful.

"This is an unexpected pleasure, Mr.
Blake. I was so sorry to hear of Van Roon's
death. You don't know how sorry I am";
he shook his head and his voice trembled.
"You don't know how sorry!"

Jimmy was surprised. He did not expect
the Minister, whose task it was to sign the
death warrants which sent men to the gallows,
to display such concern, nor did he know that
Stope-Kendrick was so close a friend of Gerald's. Stope-Kendrick secured control of his
voice after a while.

"What can I do for you?" he asked.

"I've come partly about this terrible crime, sir, and partly to ask you whether you could put me in touch with Mr. Maggerson."

The Home Secretary shook his head.

"That I am afraid I cannot do," he said. "Mr. Maggerson went away into the country after his collapse and I do not think he is get-at-able. What do you want me to tell you about the crime?"

His steady black eyes were fixed on his visitor and there was a strange look in his face; and Jimmy, who was extraordinarily sensitive to atmosphere, was impressed by the tension of the Minister's attitude.

"I can't understand, Mr. Stope-Kendrick, why the police are taking such little trouble to discover the murderer of my cousin," he said.

"It appears to you that they are taking little trouble," corrected Stope-Kendrick after a pause. "And I am afraid it always seems so to those who are interested in the solution of a mystery of this kind, but you will find that the authorities have been very active indeed. In a case like this, Mr. Blake, it is very difficult to get hold of any loose ends—

there are absolutely no clues whatever."

Jimmy was thinking rapidly. Should he tell the Home Secretary about the four visitors to the Lodge? Should he describe what he had seen through his telescope? Again he decided to maintain silence. Until he had further evidence of the nature of these meetings and the character of the men who foregathered at Blackheath he could not frame his suspicions. The explanation of these midnight visits might be a simple one. At any rate, he could do very little good at this stage by revealing all he had discovered.

Jimmy left the Home Office with a curious sense of uneasiness. He lunched at his club and there met a man who had known Gerald, and they talked of the dead man for the greater part of the afternoon.

Jimmy hung on to town desperately. He had no desire to go back to Blackheath until—he realized with a sense of comic dismay that Blake's Priory had only one attraction for him now, and that of a transitory character.

"Oh, by the way," he said at parting with the officer. "You fellows in the Guards are generally well informed. Have there been issued any very extra special secret-and-confidential-don't-tell-anybody orders during the last two days?"

The officer laughed in his face.

"And if there had been, my son, do you imagine I should whisper them into your ear?" he demanded ironically.

"But have there?" demanded Jimmy.

"Not a day passes but we do not get secret and confidential orders," said the diplomatic Guardsman.

"Have you had any printed orders?"

The soldier looked at him sharply.

"I don't know quite what you mean," he said, his tone altering.

"I mean this. You are second in command of a Guards Battalion and if there had been any very secret orders issued by the Government expressly to the military you would know all about them."

"And just as assuredly, Jimmy, you would not," said the other decidedly.

Jimmy knew, for he had served in the army, that "secret and confidential" instructions are "secret and confidential" in name only. Real secret orders were issued at the rarest intervals and dealt only with national crises. He was quite certain from Major Barrington's manner that some such order had been issued. What could it be about? Was the country expecting an attack from its late enemy, and had Schaffer's letter contained some great State secret?

"Oh damn!" said Jimmy, giving up the problem for the moment.

He was always giving it up for the moment, and returning insensibly and unconsciously to its consideration. By the rarest piece of good luck he caught sight of Delia standing at the corner of the Haymarket waiting for a 'bus. This incident was the one bright spot of the day, and he carried her off under the cold and disapproving eyes of other ladies who were waiting and in his exhilaration almost brought his Rolls into collision with a street standard.

He did not expect to find Mr. Sennett at the house, but he was there. Jimmy had insisted upon the printer using his study, and Joe rose from a welter of proofs as the young man came in.

"I'm just revising poor Mr. Van Roon's last proofs," he said. "I haven't had much time to give to the boy's books lately."

"Mr. Sennett," said Jimmy bluntly. "When did you see Maggerson last?"

Joe Sennett turned his eyes away.

"Oh, some time ago now," he drawled.

"Did you see him yesterday?"

"It is possible," said the other, and Jimmy knew he was evading the question. "Yes, I think he did call at the office." Then suddenly he dropped his mask of indifference and, turning on the astounded Jimmy: "I wish to God I knew what they were up to and what it was all about," he said, his voice trembling with anger. "They're driving me mad with their orders to troops and their mysteries—they must have allowed this poor boy to be murdered. . . ."

It was the outburst of a man whose nerve was going and Jimmy waited for more, but the old man recovered himself with a harsh laugh.

"I'm getting rattled," he said. "That is because I'm old, I suppose. Didn't I hear Delia come back with you, sir?"

Jimmy nodded.

"She must not know that anything is wrong."

"You may be sure I shall not tell her, but she'll guess," said Jimmy quietly. "She's not the kind of girl who can be easily deceived. What is wrong, Sennett?"

The old man shrugged his shoulders.

"I don't know, Mr. Blake, and I've already said too much. I'm getting a bit frightened, that is all. So is Stope-Kendrick——"

"Stope-Kendrick?" said Jimmy in wide-eyed amazement. "The Secretary of State?"

The other nodded.

"Have you seen him?" asked Jimmy incredulously.

"Yes, I've seen him." Old Joe Sennett's tone did not encourage further enquiry.

"It is killing him, whatever it is," he went on. "He looks like a dead man."

"I also saw him to-day," nodded Jimmy, "and I agree with you. He is a nice fellow too. Have you the slightest inkling in your mind what is the trouble? Is it an invasion they are scared about?"

Joe shook his head.

"I haven't the slightest idea. All I know is that certain members of the Government are in terror about something."

The Terror! Jimmy remembered Maggerson's words. But what shape was The Terror taking?

"I ought not to tell you, Mr. Blake," Joe went on, "but those secret orders which I printed were to the military commanders, ordering them to leave nothing undone to quell disturbances which may arise. It also gave them authority to shoot without the formality of reading the Riot Act. In fact, sir," he said solemnly, "the country at this moment is under a secret form of Martial Law which has been proclaimed without the people knowing anything about it. And in my opinion—" he hesitated.

"Yes?"

"In my opinion," he said soberly, "Mr. Gerald Van Roon was the first victim of that law."

Jimmy had plenty to think about that night. The girl was busy in Gerald's study, working over his letters, and he was left alone to his thoughts. He had not shuttered or curtained the window of his study. The French windows leading on to the garden were open, for it was a glorious night. He sat reading for a while until the saw the girl crossing the lawn. She had evidently finished her work, and his first impulse was to rise and go after her. Then he felt that possibly she might wish to be alone, and so he waited, alternately deciding to go and reflecting that it was better to stay, until at last he could wait no longer.

He stepped through the door of the study on to the soft carpet of the lawn. The full moon was shining and the garden was a place of mystery and inviting shadows. The shadow of a big elm lay bluely across the tennis court, throwing a big blot of darkness on the wall. There was no sound except the querulous chirp of a sleepy bird disturbed by its restless partner, and the breeze was little more than a lazy movement of air which did not so much as rustle a leaf.

He walked across the grass, stopping by the sun-dial to glance idly at the shadow which the stile cast upon the green plate. He stood for a while by the pedestal, his eyes ranging the grounds for some sign of Delia.

Beyond the elms was a stretch of garden from whence the moonlight had drawn all colour. Black straight shadows of the hollyhocks barred the wall, and the place was fragrant with rare and delicate perfumes. Then he saw her. She was sitting on a big stone bench, and he moved quicker towards her, marvelling at her nerve. The air of tragedy which lay upon the house would have shaken most women. But she could go out alone and sit, strange as it was, on poor Gerald's favourite bench.

"It is very beautiful," she said softly as he came up to her.

Jimmy thought of the garden and the lavender moonlight only as settings for her own exquisite prettiness. In this ethereal light she was wonderful to him. There was something almost unearthly in the frail modelling of her face, half-turned upwards towards him and the moon, for he stood with his own face in shade.

"You aren't catching cold?" he asked huskily.

It was a feebly maiden-auntish question to ask.

"No—won't you sit down?"

He sat and for the best part of ten minutes did not speak.

"Father may have to go to town," she broke the silence at last, and Jimmy started, for he had been dreaming the maddest, the most heart-racing dream. With difficulty he found his voice.

"Delia," he said, "I'm being rather selfish asking you to stay at the Priory. You're too young to be flung into this tragic business . . . and too dear. . . ."

Apparently she did not notice the last, for she answered steadily:

"You forget that Father likes being here. It was good of you to ask him."

Another pause.

How could he put his dream into coherent language? he wondered desperately.

"Do you like this place?" he asked.

"The house? Oh yes, it is glorious"; she dropped her voice to little more than a whisper. "Lovely . . . lovely. . . . I shall hate going back to Camberwell."

Jimmy cleared his voice as well as he could.

"Why go back?" he asked so loudly that

she turned her face towards him startled. "Why not stay. . . . I love you very truly, Delia."

Every word seemed to be exactly the word he hadn't intended using. He was crude, he thought, in a perspiration of fear.

She did not reply. She turned away from him quickly, and he saw the hands on her lap clasp and the fingers twining one about the other.

"That is impossible, Mr. Blake."

She was not looking at him, but was talking in the opposite direction.

"You . . . you are a little worried by . . . by poor Mr. Van Roon's death and . . ." She turned her head as suddenly and faced him, and her big eyes stared at him sombrely for a second, and then she laughed softly.

"It is the moonlight," she said, rising; and with a simple unaffected gesture put out her hand to him. " 'Moonlight was for fancy made,' " she quoted. "I'm going into the house and I really think I *am* a little chilled."

"One moment, Delia." Jimmy had command of his voice and himself now. "I want to say I'm sorry if I offended you, and more

sorry if you think I am not sincere or that
I am affected by the moon as other lunatics
are——"

"They're not," she smiled. "It is one of
the popular fallacies which science has ex-
ploded. And the moon has nothing to do
with the weather either——"

"Blow science," said Jimmy. "Listen to
me, Delia. I would ask you to marry me in
unromantic daylight or in a snowstorm."

The smile left her face.

"And I should say 'no,'" she answered
quietly, "though I am really touched and
grateful to you, Mr. Blake."

"You don't think you could love me?"

She shook her head.

"I think I do not love you now," she said;
"and I know that I have mapped out my life
in my humble way so that it is filled without
—without——"

"Me?"

Jimmy felt sorry for himself. His tone
was therefore a little bitter.

"Any man," she said. "Do you think I'm
not pleased—pleased and flattered beyond
your understanding?"

He was silent.

"Do you?" she persisted, shaking his arm gently. "I'm just full of gratification! I always thought women felt sorry . . . for the man when they said 'no,' or that they were uncomfortable in their minds. I think that can only be when there are two men who love them, and they want them both! But you're the one flower in my garden."

"But why?" he began bewildered.

"It's lovely to know that you're loved," she said softly. "It's selfishly lovely—but it's lovely. And I like you . . . oh, ever so much."

She drew long sigh and then:

"Come along—Jimmy," she said, and his heart leap at the word.

"I want you to like me," she went on, pacing by his side towards the house; "that is better than—more emotional feeling, isn't it? It's rare between men and women. I almost think I would sacrifice all my pet plans and half my principles to keep your liking."

Though the architecture of the Priory was Georgian, there had been erected by some former owner a large porch supported by four slender Corinthian pillars. Here were two oaken seats, on one of which Stephens the butler was wont to sit and smoke his evening pipe.

Joe Sennett had discovered the comfort of this retreat, and here they found him. The somewhat precipitate retreat of Stephens suggested that Joe had not lacked company or direction to his cosy corner.

"Hullo, Delia," growled the old man. "Isn't it time you were in bed?"

His growl was a pleasant growl, and the girl laughed.

"I'm not going to town to-morrow, Daddy. I'm staying to fix Mr. Van Roon's letters, and it's such a glorious night that I hate the idea of going to bed."

She sat down on the settle by her father's side. It was very delightful for Jim, even though it meant that he must forego for the night the plans he had made on the night before; to confront one of the visitors to the Warden's Lodge, and discover his identity. That, however, could wait, he told himself, and possibly the four would not come on so bright a night as this.

Old Joe took out his pipe and was about to speak, when there came a terrifying diversion.

It was a shriek—long and piercing—and was repeated, and it came from the direction of the Heath. The girl went white and gripped her father's arm.

"What was that?" she faltered.

Before he could reply the horrible cry sounded again, and it was coming nearer.

Jimmy tore up the drive, through the gates and out on to the deserted road. He saw a figure running towards him, its arms outflung. It was a man, and he was screaming pitifully, like a frightened child. Jim went out to meet him, but, as though at the sight of another of his kind, the runner turned and bolted away at a tangent, and all the time he shrieked and shrieked and shrieked. Jim raced after him, gaining with every stride. The man was heading for one of those deep depressions in the Heath where formerly gravel had been excavated. Suddenly he stopped on the lip of the pit and faced his pursuer.

"Don't come near me!" he yelled. "Don't come near me!"

Jim thought he recognized the voice.

"Wait, wait," he entreated, and he saw something glitter in the man's hand. There was a thunderous report and the thing that had shrieked and fled, as from the wrath of God, crumpled up and fell.

With a cry, Jim knelt by his side and turned him over. The shot must have passed through the neck, severing the spinal cord, for he was quite dead.

"My God!" breathed Jim, for he was looking at the face of John Stope-Kendrick, His Majesty's Secretary of State.

CHAPTER NINE

"WE REGRET to report the death from heart failure of the Right Honourable John Stope-Kendrick, the Home Secretary."

In this laconic manner was the suicide of John Stope-Kendrick made known to the world.

"You quite understand, Mr. Blake, that it is very undesirable the world should know the true circumstances of Mr. Stope-Kendrick's death."

Jimmy had been summoned to Downing Street for the second time and was standing in the Prime Minister's presence. The Premier seemed crushed by the tragedy which had overtaken his colleague.

"I am afraid poor Stope-Kendrick has not been quite himself for some time, but we had no idea that he was losing his mental balance." He stopped and eyed Jimmy straightly. "Mr. Blake, you and the constable who found him and the inspector and the police doctor are the only four people——"

"Mr. Sennett knows. He is a printer probably known to you," said Jimmy.

"Sennett?" said the Premier sharply. "Oh yes, of course, he is staying with you."

Jimmy wondered how the Prime Minister knew that.

"We can rely upon Mr. Sennett," said the Minister. "He prepares most of the confidential printing for the Cabinet. Nobody else knows, I hope!"

"Nobody, sir," said Jimmy promptly. At any rate he could keep the girl's name out of the matter, and he could rely upon Joe seconding him in this.

"Can you explain, sir, why Mr. Stope-Kendrick was on Blackheath at that hour of the night?"

"I cannot tell you," said the Premier. "Probably the death of poor Van Roon was on his mind, and in that case it would be very natural, if the abnormal can be natural, that he should be attracted to the spot where Van Roon was discovered. Would you accept that hypothesis?"

"It seems reasonable to me, sir," said Jimmy.

"Of course, the newspapers will know how it happened," said the Prime Minister at parting, "and possibly it will be whispered about that John died by his own hand. The great thing is that it should not be baldly and publicly stated."

"I understand, sir."

Jimmy was very grave, for only now was he sensing the bigness of the game into which he had been unconsciously drawn. He began to feel the need of a friend, and he cast his mind over the many men he knew to find one whom he could bring into his confidence. He passed them in review as he sat at his solitary lunch at the club, and rejected them all. Some lacked imagination, some, he knew, were without sympathy, some he did not like enough, and some he could not bring himself to trust in this matter. And then, when he had dismissed them and decided that he must play a lone hand, there drifted into the luncheon room a lackadaisical youth who greeted him with a feeble wave of his hand, and would have passed to another table.

It was Mr. Ferdinand Ponter, and Jimmy beckoned him.

"Come and sit down, Ferdie; I want to talk to you."

"Are you going to be frightfully intellectual?" asked the young man as he seated himself with every sign of apprehension. "The last time we met, you talked about printing till my head reeled."

"What you want," said Jimmy, "is another head. No, I'm not going to be very intellectual—yes, I am," he said suddenly, and Ferdinand's face expressed resignation and pain.

"Ferdie, I want you to help me."

"Help you," said the startled youth. "Good heavens, what do you want help for? I will, of course," he added hastily, "but I had not the slightest idea——"

"Don't be a fool; I'm not talking about money. I want you to help me in another way."

"Not about printing?" asked Mr. Ponter in alarm. "I assure you, dear old thing, I know no more about printing than I know about beeswax or Jerusalem artichokes.

Which reminds me," and he called a waiter and ordered beer with a flourish. And then, remembering suddenly that he had certain condolences to offer—"I'm awfully cut up about poor Van Roon, Jimmy," he said. "I didn't know him very well, but it must have been an awful knock in the eye for you."

"It was rather," said Jimmy shortly. "No, I'm not going to ask you about printing, Ferdie. I realize that the link between you and Ponters' is as slender as the thin edge of a cheque."

"Beautifully put," murmured the young man.

"The fact is—" Jimmy hesitated, and yet, why should he? he thought. All this boredom and lack of interest in life which Mr. Ponter expressed with every gesture and word, was a pose. Ferdie Ponter had been Jimmy's observer in the days when Jimmy drove a D.H.7. A cool child, who shot with deadly precision and never, under any circumstances, lost his nerve.

"Now, listen, I'm going to tell you a story, son, and I'm putting you on your honour that you won't mention a word of this to anybody,

whether you come in and help me or whether
you stay outside."

"You thrill me," said Ferdie.

"I shall," replied Jimmy grimly. "Now
listen to what I've got to say and don't interrupt."

He had told the story to himself so often
that he had every fact marshalled in order,
and now he presented to the gaping youth a
consecutive narrative of all that had happened from the moment Gerald Van Roon
had brought Schaffer's letter to his bedroom,
down to his latest interview with the Prime
Minister.

"Well, what do you think of it?"

Ferdie shook his head.

"I'm dashed if I know," he said. "Jehosh-
aphat! What a weird business!" and he
shook his head again.

"What do *you* think of it?" he asked.
"You know I'm not so jolly clever."

"I can't understand it," said Jimmy, "but
I'm going to learn, Ferdie; and first I shall
have a shot at the Warden's Lodge and discover what is happening there."

"That is what I was going to suggest out

of my own head!" said the other. "Have
you told anybody about Maggerson being at
the house?"

"I've told nobody. You're the first person
I've met who doesn't matter."

"Thank you very kindly," said Ferdinand
politely.

"What I mean," explained Jimmy, "is that
it will not hurt or worry you, as it would hurt
Miss Sennett."

Ferdie looked up.

"That is a name you haven't mentioned before? What the dickens are you blushing
about? Is it your fiancée, old thing? Con-
gratulations!" He pushed his paw across the
table.

"Don't be a fool," growled Jim. "It is a—
a friend staying with us, she and her father."

"Sennett," repeated Ferdie. "Why, she
isn't related to our Sennett, is she? The governor calls him our super-comp."

"She's his daughter," said Jimmy shortly.

"In-deed?" said the other interestedly.
"Are you thinking of going into the printing
trade, Jimmy?"

"As I say, I haven't told Miss Sennett because naturally she'd be worried."

"Why should she be worried if she's not your fiancée? Dash it all, old thing, be reasonable," protested Ferdie, loath to part with his theory.

"Huxley said," quoted Jimmy severely, "that the greatest tragedy in science is to see a beautiful hypothesis killed by an ugly fact —she is *not* my fiancée."

"I wouldn't call you ugly," murmured Ferdinand, somewhat at sea; "and who's Huxley?"

"That's beside the point," said Jimmy, who was growing uncomfortably hot. "What I want to know is, will you stand in with me, if I make an attempt to enter this lodge and discover what was behind the killing of poor Jerry and the suicide of Stope-Kendrick?"

"I'm with you all the time," said Ferdie, and solemnly shook hands. "I've been wondering what I was going to do for the next week or two. I'm engaged for the Ascot week, of course; and I may pop down to Epsom for the Derby; but, with the exception

of the Derby, I haven't a single engagement.
All my girls have shaken me, I'm frightfully
unpopular with the paternal authority, I've
overdrawn my allowance to a terrific extent,
and I wish I were dead!"

"Probably if you accompany me on this
little job your wish will be gratified," said
Jimmy unpleasantly, and Ferdie bright-
ened up.

He had theories too; immediate and start-
ling. Though no student, Ferdie was a reader
and an admirer of literature in which mysteries abound, and where the villain of the
piece is always the last person to be suspected
by the reader. Therefore, Ferdie cast his
eyes and his mind around for those who had
the best credentials of innocence, and he suspected in turn the Prime Minister, Stephens,
the butler, old Mr. Sennett, and he was on
the point of naming Delia, when Jimmy fixed
him with a steely eye.

"Maggerson's in it, of course," Ferdie
prattled on. "Up to his eyebrows. And that
old German Johnnie Schaffer—why don't
you send Schaffer a wire and ask him what
his nonsensical letter was all about?"

Jimmy stared at him.

"Out of the mouths of babes and sucklings," he said admiringly. "I never thought of that!"

There was no difficulty in locating Professor Schaffer. The first telephone enquiry Jimmy put through, which was to a friend of Gerald's, discovered the Professor's address, and a long wire phrased in German was despatched to Leipzig without delay.

Jimmy was driving home that night satisfied with the day's work, and had reached the southern end of Westminster Bridge on his way to Blackheath, when a newspaper poster attracted his eye. It was the placard of a Labour journal, bitterly antagonistic to the Government, but of this Jimmy was not aware. All he saw was the sensational announcement in the biggest type:

"Weltman goes mad."

He pulled up the car with a jerk, jumped out and snatched a newspaper. Lord Harry Weltman. The *bête noire* of all Labour men and the third member of that fatal party at Downing Street! Mad!

CHAPTER TEN

LORD HARRY WELTMAN was a singular example of how a man may achieve success in spite of the most hampering disadvantages. The story of the poor and comparatively humble office boy who starts life with a shilling, and by the application of his genius to his employers' affairs, rises to such heights that he is in a position to make his former master a small allowance to keep him from starvation, is a common enough instance in the biographies of the great. But Lord Harry Weltman had succeeded in spite of the fact that he was the third son of an impecunious duke. Handicapped by his aristocratic associations, he had outraged the feelings of his lordly family by going into business at eighteen, and had built up one of the largest industries in Great Britain. He was the part-inventor and the complete exploiter of the "Stael Six," a motor-car that had made history. He had gradually drawn into his control other motor-car firms, and as his wealth increased, had bought up huge blocks of land which his discerning eye had marked for future townships.

There was scarcely a great city throughout the kingdom on the outskirts of which he had not acquired land, and his purchases were justified, for it was in the direction of his holdings that the towns invariably grew.

At forty-eight he was a multi-millionaire, the pride and envy of his ducal brother. At fifty-six he was a Cabinet Minister. He was a hard man, and the mention of his name at a Labour meeting was invariably received with groans. His inclusion in the Cabinet had been one of the most courageous acts of the Prime Minister's life, and for a while seriously imperilled his administration.

Weltman was a stickler for his pound of flesh. He ground from his workmen the very last ounce of energy for which he paid them. Rent day for his cottagers was a day of judgment, for inexorable were his demands, and inevitable were the consequences of non-payment.

He was a just man, and justice and popularity can never go hand in hand. In one respect he baffled his detractors. If he demanded his rents on the day and the hour they were due, his tenants were better treated in the matter of repairs and hygienic equipment than were most. And their rents were reasonably low. If he fought strikes, he also fought the disease which is so prevalent in congested industrial areas. His factories were planned for the safety and comfort of his workers; no safeguard which science could suggest or knowledge install had been left unplaced. His mines were the best equipped in the country, and the living conditions of the miners infinitely superior in comfort to their fellows employed in other mines.

The office of Weltman's Consolidated Industries, through which holding-company Lord Harry controlled his interests, was in Throgmorton Street; an unpretentious building of three floors. Since his elevation to Cabinet rank Lord Harry had paid very few visits to the City, but on the morning of Kendrick's death he descended from his electric brougham at the door and was ushered into the little office which he occupied when he had occasion to give his personal attention to his multifarious investments.

The General Secretary, a man who had grown grey in his service, and who had never ceased to be nervous in his presence, met him at the door and led the way to the sanctum.

Lord Harry lounged in, took off his gloves leisurely, his eyes all the time upon the neat pile of papers on his desk.

"You have made the summaries, Johnson?" he asked in his harsh voice.

"Yes, my Lord," said the grey Johnson. "I have set all the properties, their rents, etc., in one list. This," he pointed to the other pile, "are the salary sheets summarized as your Lordship suggested."

Lord Harry grunted something and seated himself at the desk.

"And this is the Power of Attorney." He took up a sheet of paper. "Bring in two witnesses."

Two scared clerks appeared, and when Lord Harry had signed the instrument, attested their names and were dismissed with a nod.

"Now understand, Johnson, what I am doing. The day after to-morrow is pay day,
and every man employed by me is to receive
the equivalent of three years' salary, by way
of bonus. If he has not been in my employ
three years, then he will receive a bonus
equivalent to the salary which he has already
drawn. This applies to the office staff. So
far as you are concerned, you will draw a
cheque for yourself equivalent to fifteen
years' salary."

"Oh, my Lord . . ." began the fluttered
Johnson.

"Don't interrupt, please," snapped Lord
Harry. "I also asked you to prepare an omni-
bus deed of gift, setting forth the names of all
my tenants and their properties. I am trans-
ferring my cottages to their present tenants."

"I have it here, my Lord." Mr. Johnson
found the document and laid it before Lord
Harry with a trembling hand. "I hope your
Lordship won't mind my saying that this extraordinary generosity on your part takes my
breath away. Your Lordship realizes that
this will cost you the greater part of a million
and a half."

"I am worth about three times that, am I not?" asked Lord Harry. "The only worry I have in my mind," he said thoughtfully as he looked out of the window, "is whether I am giving enough. You see, Johnson, I have been working very hard and very uselessly, it seems to me. After a man has sufficient food to eat, and a roof over his head, a car to ride in, and sufficient for his living and pleasure, the additional money is dead money unless it is employed for the general benefit. I am going to give eight thousand people a great deal of happiness, Johnson. If I thought that it would double their happiness by doubling the grant I made them, I should certainly double it."

He brought his head round and met Johnson's bewildered look, and a little smile played at the corner of his thin lips.

"I hope your Lordship doesn't mind my asking you, but is this matter to be made public?"

Lord Harry nodded.

"I want our people to know as soon as possible, and I can think of no better way than through the public press. Moreover," he hesitated, "I may induce other employers to do the same. I think I could too," he added slowly. "Now let me have the deed of gift."

Again the two clerks were brought in and the document was signed and witnessed. Then Lord Harry got up from his chair and looked round the office.

"I've had some very interesting times in this office, Johnson. I suppose you have too!"

"Yes, my Lord, I've had some very happy times here," admitted Mr. Johnson; and Lord Harry wondered what happiness there could be in servitude.

Two hours later every newspaper throughout the country had the story. The Labour journals had only one explanation for this munificence of Lord Harry Weltman and issued the placard which Jimmy saw.

He read the two columns from start to finish and then tucked the paper away by the side of the seat.

Weltman had certainly gone mad, but it was a very pleasant and admirable form which his derangement took.

Delia was standing under the porch when he drove up and she looked worried.

"I've had a note from Father saying he will not be home to-night—" she laughted in spite of herself. "It is queer how easily I'm calling the Priory 'home.' I almost feel that I have lived here all my life."

"To which I could make an admirable rejoinder," said Jimmy.

"Well, don't," she said promptly.

"Where is your father staying?" he asked her, taking her arm and leading her into the garden.

"At our house in Camberwell," she replied. "He says he will stay there when he is not at the office. He has so much work to do, that he will not have time to come to Blackheath. Did you talk to the Prime Minister?"

He nodded.

"And what did he say about that poor gentleman?"

"Kendrick? Nothing. He asked me whether you knew."

"I?" she said in surprise.

"Apparently he knows that you and your father are my guests. I told him that you knew nothing and had seen nothing."

She was silent.

"I'm becoming so confused," she said at last. "I feel that something very dreadful is happening. I know the death of poor Mr. Van Roon was terrible in itself, and so was that awful—awful—" her lips trembled and she shivered, but she mastered her distress, and went on steadily. "But they seem to me to be incidents in a bigger and a more catastrophic disaster. Tell me, Mr. Blake"—she looked him straight in the eyes—"is there any likelihood of war?"

He shook his head.

"So far as I know we are at peace with the world," he said. "Even the French are speaking well about us, and they haven't done that since July, 1914. No, I can't imagine there is going to be a war. In many ways I wish there were; it would be something definite."

She nodded.

"That is how I feel."

They paced the gravel path in silence. She walked with her hands clasped behind her, her eyes on the ground.

"The plant has nothing to do with the trouble?" she said, apropos of nothing.

"The plant?"

"Don't you remember Mr. Maggerson brought a plant. I asked Father if he had heard anything about a strange plant which Mr. Maggerson brought home from Mexico. He told me that Mr. Maggerson had not brought a specimen to England. It had died on the voyage and was thrown overboard by a steward who did not know its value."

"I always thought that was too fantastic a theory," said Jimmy; but he was rather glad that the mysterious plant had been disposed of.

"But isn't the whole thing fantastic?" she asked. "Isn't it fantastic that a man like your cousin, who hadn't a single enemy in the world, should be butchered almost within sight of your house? Isn't it fantastic that Mr. Kendrick, who was a deeply religious man—I have been reading his biography in the newspaper this morning—should have taken his own life?"

Jimmy could not answer this. The whole thing was maddening. There was no thread which led anywhere. He touched the broken ends of a tangled skein.

"Isn't it fantastic that my father should be brought into this matter?" she added.

"That isn't fantastic at all," said Jimmy quietly. "Your father happens to be the foreman compositor of a firm of Government printers. The fact that they also print scientific work is a coincidence. It is natural, therefore, that he should be in the business, if not of it. No, Delia, even Ferdie Ponter doesn't think that that is fantastic."

She looked at him quickly.

"Ponter? That is the name of the house for whom Father works. You know the son, don't you?"

Jimmy told her of his conversation with Ferdie at the club.

"He isn't a bad fellow; really he's quite a plucky kid. I must have somebody with me in this."

She stopped dead and looked at him in perplexity.

"You must have somebody with you?" she repeated slowly. "Why? What are you doing?"

"I'm going to find who killed Gerald Van Roon and why Kendrick shot himself. I'm going to discover the mystery of the—" he stopped himself in time. He was on the point of revealing all he knew about the Warden's Lodge.

"The mystery of what?"

"One or two minor mysteries," he said carelessly. "They've all got to be cleared up. I can foresee, Delia, that I shall come through this crisis a very high-class intelligence officer."

"Suppose you don't come through?" She asked the question quietly.

The idea had never occurred to Jimmy before.

"Do you imagine that people who did not hesitate to kill your cousin, and who drove a Cabinet Minister to suicide, would think twice before they removed you?"

Jimmy scratched his nose.

"You're full of cheerful thoughts this evening, Delia. Anyway, Ferdie is coming over to sleep to-night," he said, to change the subject. "I've asked him to come in time for dinner. He plays bezique, so we shall be able to amuse ourselves after you have retired."

"I'm not going to bed very early to-night," she said calmly, "and it will be much easier to tell me what are your plans, than to devise methods for getting rid of me."

But Jimmy did not accept the invitation.

Ferdie came roaring up the drive in his racing Italia just before dinner, and naturally he brought half-a-dozen new theories, all of which had to be discussed in the girl's absence.

Ferdie was frankly relieved when he discovered that the daughter of his father's foreman was presentable.

"Why, my dear Jimmy," he said reproachfully, "she's pretty."

"Did I say she wasn't?" growled Jimmy.

"You old dog," said the admiring Ferdie, "keeping that secret from your innocent friend! Why, Jimmy, she's *lovely!*"

"Now, suppose we discuss something else," said Jimmy rudely. "Have you brought the things I asked you to get?"

Ferdie nodded.

"They're in the car," he said. "Rope with a large hook, telescopic ladder, two perfectly good electric torches. Shall I bring 'em in?"

"Don't be a fool," said Jimmy violently.

"What do you want to bring them in for? Let me impress upon you, before we go any farther, Ferdie, that this job is dangerous."

"So I gathered," said the complacent youth. "In fact, I've always understood that burglary was the most unhealthy profession a chap could follow."

"This isn't burglary," insisted Jimmy.

"It's very much like it," said Ferdie, "but that doesn't worry me. I'll be over the wall in a jiffy——"

"You'll not go over the wall at all," said Jimmy emphatically. "I am going over; your job is to keep watch, and stow away the ladder so that some cycling policeman doesn't discover it, and stand by in case of accidents."

"What do you expect to find in the Warden's Lodge?"

"If I had the slightest idea of what I expected, I shouldn't probably attempt to investigate," said Jimmy.

"Which is jolly cryptic," nodded Ferdinand, and went on to apologize. "Cryptic is a word which I learnt last week, old thing; I hope you don't mind my trying it on you."

Jimmy looked at his watch.

"There is time to go to the garage and transfer those things to my car, which is a little less noisy than yours. Have you any arms?"

"And legs, old bird," said Ferdie promptly, "a well-balanced head and a pair of reasonable feet."

"Fire-arms, you goop!" snarled Jimmy impatiently.

But these Ferdie had not brought.

"You needn't worry," said Jimmy. "I've a couple of automatics upstairs and there's plenty of ammunition in the gun-room."

"Do you really anticipate bloodshed?" asked Ferdie hopefully. "I've got a couple of old Mills bombs at home that I brought back from France."

"And you can keep them at home," said Jimmy. "I hope there's going to be no shooting, which means that I hope nobody is going to shoot me. If I meet any person who shows the slightest inclination to bring my agreeable life to an end, there'll be a sharp exchange of repartee."

"Good for you," said Ferdie, "and I'll dash over the wall and bring your body back, and——"

At that moment the door opened and Delia came hurriedly into the study.

"What is wrong?" asked Jimmy quickly after a glance at her face.

"Will you come, please, Mr. Blake?"

He joined her in the passage.

"Has anything happened?"

"I saw Tom Elmers—you remember the man?"

"Saw him, where?"

"He was in the garden," said the girl. "I saw him going into the shrubbery."

It was nearly dark, but there was light enough to make a search without the aid of lanterns.

"He looked awful," she told him. "I don't think you had better go. I think he is mad too."

"Did he see you?"

She nodded.

"He spoke to me—he—he asked the strangest questions—what had happened to Mr. Maggerson, and——"

She covered her face with her hands and shuddered.

"He looked dreadful—dreadful," she

whispered. "Please do not go, Mr. Blake."

But Jimmy was half-way across the garden, heading for the shrubbery. He had no weapons but his hands and it never occurred to him that he would need them. The first intimation of danger came with a shrill swish from behind him, and he leapt forward into a laurel bush. The stick just missed him, and he heard a thud as it struck the ground and a crack as it broke. Then he turned to grapple with his attacker. In the half-light he would not have recognized the man, for Elmers's face was red and more bloated, and the hair about his chin and mouth was long and unkempt. Jim warded the blow the man aimed at him and then gripped him, but only for a second. Jimmy was prepared for the blow, but not for the kick that followed. The man's boot struck his shin, and he released his hold; in that moment his assailant had wriggled out of his grip and flown along the path. By the time Jimmy limped up, he was astride the wall.

"I'll get her and I'll get Joe, too; you tell her that! I know all about Joe. I know all about Maggerson!" he yelled.

"You'll know all about me if you come down here, you swine!" said Jimmy between his teeth; and then; stooping quickly, he picked up a stone and flung it, and Mr. Elmers's interest in the Sennett family would have suffered a total eclipse, if he had not, with a lightning wriggle, dropped to the other side of the wall.

CHAPTER ELEVEN

JIMMY went back to the house, and Delia's concern and sorrow, Delia's swift flight for hot water and cotton wool and iodine, Delia's almost motherly treatment of a sore shin, made Tom Elmers a respectable member of society and a daily encounter with him something to be looked forward to.

"It might have broken a bone," said the girl in a hushed voice. "You ought to go straight to bed, Mr. Blake."

Jimmy exchanged glances with Ferdie.

"I'm sorry I can't go to bed," said Jimmy meekly; "I have an important Board Meeting to-night—not a Board Meeting—I mean a——"

"A little supper party," suggested Ferdie helpfully.

She looked grave.

"Are you going on this—adventure?" she asked.

"It is not so much an adventure, Miss Sennett," interrupted Ferdie. "It's a little look round. Don't you be worried about him. I'll bring him back safe and sound."

"Miss Sennett isn't worried about me," said Jim coldly. "She is no more interested in my coming back safe and sound than she is about you."

Ferdie's young face went blank with astonishment.

"Ain't you engaged?" he asked in surprise, and that was his crowning indiscretion of the evening.

"But, my dear old thing, you call her by her Christian name" (this in the privacy of the study five minutes later). "I thought she was a great friend of yours; and really the Florence Nightingale way she bandaged your hairy old leg——"

"You're an ass, Ferdie," wailed Jimmy. "Don't you see how unfortunate your remark was? You've made her feel very uncomfortable."

"Suppose I go and apologize to her?"

"Suppose you don't," said Jimmy. "You

just sit where you are, Ferdie. You've done enough mischief for one day."

The soreness to his shin remained, but by practice he found that it did not impede his power of locomotion, though it might conceivably affect him when he came to climbing. He was determined to make his attempt that night, and it seemed that the girl was equally determined that he should not. He dropped all pretence of having an engagement and went about the task of sitting her out.

By half-past twelve everybody was yawning except Delia, who was cool and as fresh as though she had wakened from a long and dreamless sleep.

"It is late; I shall go to bed," said Jimmy desperately at last, and made a significant sign to his fellow-conspirator.

"I think that is a very excellent idea, Mr. Blake," said Delia calmly. "You don't know how safe I feel here with you and Mr. Ponter in the house. I think if I woke up in the night and heard your car going off I should faint from sheer terror."

"Oh yes," said Jimmy uncomfortably.

"Then, you see, we've no intention of going out, have we, Ferdie?"

"None whatever," said Mr. Ponter glibly.

When Jimmy woke up the next morning with his leg so stiff that he could hardly bear his weight upon it, he was grateful that the girl had had her way. He was not feeling at all easy about Tom Elmers. The man was in the neighbourhood, and the knowledge of this fact had been a stronger argument for not leaving Delia alone than any she had offered. He did not for one moment imagine that she would fall into a panic if he left her alone in the house, for "alone" was a term which implied in this case the protection of two maid-servants, a valet, and a butler.

He hobbled down to breakfast late. Ferdie, who had preceded him by only a few minutes, cast a reproachful glance in his direction.

"Jimmy, you're going to be late for church," he said.

"For church?" said Jimmy in amazement. "Is it Sunday?"

"Of course it's Sunday." Delia looked at him reprovingly as she filled his cup.

"And Mr. Ponter has very kindly offered to take me to church."

"How sweet of Mr. Ponter!" said Jimmy savagely. "Good Lord, Sunday!"

"Don't you ever go to church?" she asked severely.

"Frequently."

"Well, you're coming this morning, of course?" she said. "The Bishop of Fleet is preaching at St. Gregory's."

Jimmy looked at her.

"The Bishop of what?"

"The Bishop of Fleet."

The name vividly recalled the luncheon party at Downing Street.

"He was one of the fellows at the Prime Minister's party," explained Jimmy. "What the dickens is he doing so far out of his diocese? What is the matter, Ferdie?"

Mr. Ferdinand Ponter was frowning.

"The Bishop of Fleet? That's old Stillman! He was the head of my school. Squirrel, we called him. Good Lord, I can't go and hear him spout theology. The mere mention of his name makes a cold shiver go down my spine."

"He was head, was he?" said Jimmy, interested. "Was he strong on the classical side?"

Ferdie shook his head.

"He was the most horribly modern person you could meet," he said. "Specialized in bugs and isms; he was a terror to the sixth —he took us in science."

"That accounts for his acquaintance with Maggerson and the Prime Minister," nodded Jimmy. "I'd like to hear this gentleman."

"He'll terrify you," warned Ferdie.

"Not he!" said Jimmie confidently. "There isn't an ex-headmaster in the world, bar one, that could put fear into my brave heart."

"This is the one *I* bar," said Ferdie, "but I'll go."

He looked at Delia and nodded.

"I'll go."

St. Gregory's Church was reputedly "high." It was one to which Churchmen who were not so high went regularly to count the candles and to scoff at the incense.

Jimmy was a public school boy, which meant that he attended chapel regularly every day of his life for years and years, until he left the University, when he went to church no more, regarding religious observances as part of a very painful discipline. But he had never had the peculiarly sweet experience of sitting elbow to elbow with a neat-tailored figure, or of listening to her sweet voice singing the responses, nor had he felt the spiritual uplift which can only come to man when he sees the woman he loves at prayers. He settled back in his pew as a heavy figure climbed slowly to the pulpit. It was the cleric he had seen at 10 Downing Street; less jovial; melancholy rather, for with his face in repose the Bishop's lips drooped.

He gave out a text in a voice so low that Jimmy could not hear it and consulted the girl in a whisper. She shook her head.

There was nothing in the sermon that was in any way striking. It was a carefully reasoned, beautifully phrased appeal for human charity and loving-kindness; and it was not until the end was approaching and when the congregation had braced its feet to rise for the Benediction, that he leant over the edge of the pulpit and spoke in a new and a tremulous voice. What he was saying, Jimmy could not gather. It was a wild appeal for the unity of man with man, for charity in all dealings, for love in all relationships, for the casting out of all hate and prejudices; and, as he progressed, his words grew wilder, his sentences more involved. Once he stopped for a word, stammered and went on; his voice grew thinner and shriller until it was a wail. The congregation stirred uneasily; people were looking from the Bishop to one another; then, to the consternation of everybody, this big, healthy man broke down utterly, and laying his head upon his arms, sobbed like a child.

Jimmy was on his feet. It was a note he had heard before, that thin tone of fear. It was the note in poor Kendrick's voice. Then his face went white. He was hardly conscious of the fact that the girl's hand was in his and that she was pulling at him.

"Sit down, sit down!" He heard her faintly and fell back heavily in the pew.

He felt dulled, numbed, incapable of receiving any further impression. He stirred as the church wardens gathered about the pulpit in the deathly and painful silence broken only by the Bishop's sobs; and then the organ thundered out and the tension was broken. They joined the throng in the aisle, and Delia breathed a sigh of relief when they reached the open air.

CHAPTER TWELVE

BY THE KING A PROCLAMATION

WHEREAS it is desirable that members of one family should from time to time come together for the re-establishment of those bonds of affection and service which are the bases on which the fabric of nationality is erected; and

WHEREAS many citizens of this realm, by reason of their pecuniary circumstance and the incidence of their toil, are unable to foregather periodically with their relatives; and

WHEREAS it is desirable that opportunity should be given for the stimulation of the amenities of family life;

NOW therefore I, John Henry Felbent, Earl of Morland and Tynewood, President of His Majesty's Most Honourable Privy Council, declare that the 15th and 16th days of May shall be celebrated as a public holiday and shall be known and styled, "The Days of Uniting." And it is declared that on the 15th day of May, free transportation shall be given over the railway systems of this realm and all other public conveyances and transportation services. And that on the 16th day of May all transportation and labour of all kinds shall cease for a period of twenty-four hours."

Jimmy read the announcement in bed. "The Days of Uniting!" He dressed, and came down, to find Ferdie and Delia had read the news and were speculating upon its significance.

"What I want to know is this," said Ferdie querulously. "Does this mean I've got to call on my Aunt Rachel, or must Aunt Rachel call on me? It looks to me like a plot to get me to one of her beastly dinners at Hindhead."

Delia looked up as Jimmy came in and nodded. He had gone to bed early the previous night, abandoning his contemplated search of the Warden's Lodge, all the more readily because there was a bright moon which made the night wholly unsuitable for his purpose.

"I can't understand it a little bit," he said. "Everything seems to have grown out of that fatal luncheon. Do you realize that of the dozen people who were there, two are dead, one is broken, another has performed the eccentric feat of giving away his money, Maggerson has disappeared——"

"Who is broken? You mean the Bishop?" asked Delia.

Jimmy nodded.

"That's where you're mistaken, old bean," said Ferdinand triumphantly. "I met the Squirrel this morning. He was bicycling and the old de—gentleman recognized me, and was as hearty and as cheerful as you could wish, Jimmy!"

"Did he say anything about his breakdown yesterday?"

"Yes, he even had the audacity to talk about overwork," said Ferdie. "That fellow has a memory like a cash register! He recalled both whackings he gave me—devilish bad taste, I think."

"Did he whack you?" asked Jimmy with a faint smile. "My respect for him increases."

"Mr. Ponter says that the Bishop was quite himself," said Delia.

"What are you doing up this morning so early?" asked Jimmy, pushing aside his egg; and Ferdie smiled triumphantly.

"Making a reconnaissance. Also chasing a gentleman I saw in the garden at daybreak."

The girl turned her startled face to his.

"You never told me about that."

"The fact is, Miss Delia, I suffer from overwhelming modesty," he confessed. "I didn't intend telling you. A terrible ruffian he was too; I shouldn't have heard him, but my window looks out on to the leads, and just as it was getting light I heard somebody working away at my window—and he was the clumsiest burglar I have ever heard about. I got up, and there was the gentleman trying to push up the bottom sash with the aid of a pocket-knife. The moment he saw me he bolted, slipped down to the ground and was half-way across the garden before I could get going. I dressed myself more or less sketchily, and went to look for him."

"What sort of a man was he?"

"About your height, Jimmy. Fairly young, with vile whiskers and a boozy face."

Jimmy and Delia exchanged glances. They knew it was the half-mad Elmers who had been seeking an entrance to the house.

After breakfast Jimmy led his friend into the study.

"If you have any exciting adventures ashore or afloat, that you would care to relate, I should be pleased if you would keep them for my private ear," he said unkindly. "I do not wish Miss Sennett to be alarmed."

"I'm dreadfully sorry, Jimmy," said the penitent Ferdie. "I really didn't intend talking at all—it was your idiotic question as to what I was doing out so early in the morning which was the cause of the revelation. Who is he, anyway?"

"He was recently an employee of your papa," said Jimmy, and Ferdie saw light.

"Is that the fellow who messed about with old Van Roon's type?"

Jimmy nodded.

"To-night we'll have a look at the Warden's Lodge, Ferdie," he said, "but I must
go alone. I can't leave the girl by herself.
This Elmers person is obviously half mad,
and I am a little scared for her sake. In
fact, I am beginning to think that Blackheath
is a pretty unhealthy neighbourhood."

"I've always told you so," said the complacent Ferdie. "Give me jolly old Caven-
dish Square, that's quite rural enough for
me."

Before they put their plans into operation
that night, Jimmy told the girl frankly just
what he intended doing.

"The Warden's Lodge?" she said in surprise. "Is that the house behind the wall?"

"That is the place," said Jimmy.

"But surely you do not connect the death
of Mr. Van Roon, or the suicide of Mr. Kendrick with the Lodge?"

He nodded.

"But how?"

"That's just the information I can't give
you," he said. "I tell you I'm as uncertain
and doubtful about this aspect of the mystery

as I am about the whole business. I shall
leave Ferdie with you and make my attempt
alone."

"You'll do nothing of the sort," she said
quietly. "I shall not go to bed, and you can
tell your men-servants to be about until you
return." She bit her lip thoughtfully. "I
wish I could get into touch with Father."

"You haven't heard from him?"

She shook her head.

"I think he must be engaged on very important work—oh, of course," she said suddenly. "He printed the Proclamation!"

"The Days of Uniting!" said Jimmy in
surprise. "Of course, they would have to
print posters."

"They are stuck up all over the town,"
said Ferdie. "I saw one pasted on the wall
of Greenwich Park, and two on each side of
the gates."

"That is it," said the girl, relieved. "So
it wasn't so mysterious after all. I expect
we shall see him to-day."

But the night did not bring old Sennett,
nor any word from him.

Though Jimmy had his doubts as to the

wisdom of leaving her, she insisted on his taking Ferdinand; and at half-past eleven the big Rolls slipped silently from the drive, and, taking a circuitous route, came slowly along the road by the Park and stopped near the Warden's Lodge. It was a night suitable for their purpose, for the weather had broken again and rain was falling drearily.

Ferdie carried the collapsible ladder and the rope from the body of the car, and laid them on the grass some distance from the road, where they would be free from the observation of passing travellers.

The difficulty was the disposal of the car. That difficulty was ended by driving on to the Heath and leaving it, trusting to luck that nobody strayed in that direction and, scenting a mystery in the abandoned car, communicated with the police.

Both men were in dark raincoats, and they were very necessary, though, as it proved, somewhat inadequate. They had not been waiting an hour before Jimmy was uncomfortably wet.

About twenty past twelve the light of a

car appeared, stopped at the usual distance, and after a while turned.

"Here is the first of the conspirators," said Jimmy. "They're as regular as the German artillery!"

It was the man with a stick who came first that night, walking slowly, and he turned into the house only a little ahead of the second man, whose car appeared immediately after the first had turned.

"Here's number three, the cyclist," whispered Jimmy. "He's going to burn his light to-night. No, he isn't, he's put it out."

The cyclist came noiselessly from the murk and followed his two companions.

"Now for the fourth," said Jimmy, but he waited in vain. The fourth man did not appear.

The explanation came to Jimmy with a flash and took his breath away.

"Ferdie!" he whispered, "there will be no fourth to-night."

"Why not?" asked Ferdie.

"Because he's dead," said Jimmy. "The fourth man was Stope-Kendrick!"

"You're wrong, my lad," hissed Ferdie. "There he is! Get down!"

They crouched, for the new man was walking on the grass, on their side of the road. His behaviour was peculiar. He did not go through the gate, although he went up to it, and they heard a faint squeak as he tried the handle.

"Can you see him?" whispered Ferdie.

Jimmy nodded.

"Perhaps he's forgotten the key," whispered Ferdie again, but Jimmy pressed his arm to enjoin silence.

They heard the swish of something being thrown. What was happening they could not see. Only occasionally did Jimmy detect the bulk of the black figure against a background almost as dark. Then he focussed his night glasses. The figure seemed taller than it did before, and a second later was even taller; the new-comer was climbing the wall! They heard the squeak of the iron *chevaux de frise* as they turned in their sockets, and saw the mystery man's head disappear into the greater darkness of the background above the wall. There was no skyline for them.

Behind were the chestnut trees, and what was happening they could only conjecture.

They waited a few minutes, and then they heard a soft thud.

"He has got to the other side," whispered Ferdie excitedly; and, standing up, they stepped gingerly across the road towards the wall. A rope was hanging from the iron spikes at the top.

"That's queer," said Jimmy. "Perhaps he did forget his key, but if he'd forgotten his key, he wouldn't have thought to bring the rope."

Jimmy was in a dilemma. If the man who went over was one of the four he might follow, taking the risks he had anticipated. If, on the other hand, the man was an interloper, some stray burglar who, for reasons best known to himself, was paying the Lodge a visit, the chance of detection was doubled.

"We'll wait for an hour," he said. "If nothing happens then, we'll go over."

At the end of half an hour Ferdie clutched his arm.

"Did you hear that?" he demanded under his breath.

It was the crash of glass they had heard, then:

"Joe! If it's you, come and fight, you old devil!"

The words were not spoken in anything higher than a conversational tone and came apparently from the other side of the wall and near at hand.

"Elmers," gasped Jimmy. "Listen, he is coming this way."

They heard feet in the garden, and then a shot broke through the silence of the night. There was no other sound.

"What do you think is happening?" whispered Ferdie.

"Maybe they're reading the Proclamation to him," said Jimmy grimly.

They waited another half an hour, and then:

"I'm going over," he said.

The collapsible ladder was a simple affair, and in half a minute they had laid the top rung against the spikes and Jimmy had mounted. He could see nothing. There was no light visible, nor, peering down, could he discover a secure place to drop. He negotiated the spikes and discovered they were not as formidable as they appeared from the roadway. They served their purpose too, for he hooked the end of the rope he carried to one of the rusty iron supports, and let himself slide down on the other side of the wall.

He came to earth on a heap of garden refuse, the same that probably had broken the fall of Tom Elmers, if Tom Elmers it was.

The garden was choked with laurel bushes, but his electric lamp showed him a weed-grown path, and this he followed.

Though the house was not more than fifty feet from the road, it was a considerable time before he sighted it. It was in darkness, and there was no sign of life. He walked round to the back, and here he was rewarded. A light was showing from a small window, but it was not this which brought him to a standstill, holding his breath.

At the back of the house there was a space clear of trees. Here, on what appeared to be a lawn, three or four men were working. It was when he discovered the nature of their labour, that his heart came into his mouth.

They were digging a hole. Presently the man who was in the hole stopped and climbed wearily forth; and then the three lifted something that was on the ground, and placed it in the earth. It was the body of a man; Jimmy had no doubts as to whose body it was. He moved closer, lying flat on the grass, and worming his way forward. Somebody was talking in a deep emotional voice, and the curious intonation puzzled him, until he realized that the speaker was reading the Burial Service!

Jimmy was incapable of further movement. He could only lie staring at the blurred figures which loomed through the rain, standing over the grave of the man they had killed. He heard the chik-chik of earth against steel spades. They were filling in the hole.

Tom Elmers was dead! Who had shot him? Was it Sennett? He thought he had recognized the bowed figure of old Joe climbing out of the grave, but the light was bad and so uncertain that he could not be sure. After a while their labours were finished and they moved in the direction of the house and disappeared.

Jimmy waited for a long time before he dared move, and then, pulling off his boots and tying the laces together so that he could sling them round his neck, he stepped cautiously towards the lighted window.

It must have been half an hour after the burial before he manœuvred himself so that he could look into the room without fear of detection. The light, he found afterwards, came from a tin kerosene lamp, which had a reflector; and it was not until the lamp was turned, so that no direct light was shining towards the window, that he raised his head and looked.

There were five men in the room. Maggerson he recognized at once. He was sitting at a table covered with papers, and he was writing for dear life. Opposite to him was a stranger, whom Jimmy did not remember to have seen before—a tall, grey-bearded man. He also was writing with a pencil, apparently taking no notice of his fellow-scribe.

Another man was sweeping the room. A

cigar was clenched between his teeth, and he was sweeping with long, slow, methodical strokes. He turned his head, and Jimmy nearly swooned. It was the Prime Minister of England! And the man who was holding the dust-pan was Joe Sennett.

That was not the last of his surprises. A small fire was burning in an old-fashioned grate. The fifth person was bending over the fire frying bacon. The aroma of it came to Jimmy as he stood. Here, then, was a fitting companion to the picture of the Prime Minister of England sweeping a floor; for the cook was the Lord Bishop of Fleet.

Jimmy gazed fascinated.

Presently the bacon was done, and the Bishop, who wore his apron and his gaiters —Jimmy noticed that his boots were wet and muddy—took up a coffee-pot and filled the cups on the sideboard; and then faintly the watcher heard him say:

"This man's death must be registered."

"Registered!" said the Prime Minister's voice in the deepest scorn. "My dear Frederick, don't be absurd!"

·   ·   ·   ·   ·

Jimmy pulled up the rope after him and came down the ladder slowly.

"What did you see?" whispered Ferdie, agog with excitement.

"Nothing," said Jimmy. "Get the car while I fold this ladder, Ferdie."

"But you must have seen something," urged Ferdie as the car was making its noiseless way across the Heath.

"Nothing, except—Elmers is dead."

"I thought so," Ferdie nodded. "And what else did you discover?"

"What sort of a mind must a man have," asked Jimmy slowly, "to read the Burial Service over a man he has helped murder, and to follow the performance by frying bacon?"

Ferdie looked at him in alarm.

"Don't say you have gone off your jolly old head!" he asked anxiously.

"No, I haven't gone off my jolly old head," replied Jimmy, rousing himself; "and for heaven's sake don't give Miss Sennett the impression that I have. Now remember, Ferdie Ponter," he said as he stopped the car

just outside the house, "you're not to say anything about the shot, or Elmers!"

"Was it the—er—deceased Elmers?"

"That was the gentleman."

"The fellow who tried to break in last
night?"

Jimmy nodded.

"Oh well," said Ferdie, relieved, "he ain't
very important, is he?"

Delia had arranged to wait up for them
in the study, and her look of relief when they
appeared was especially gratifying to Jimmy.

"Did you make any discovery?" was the
first question she asked.

"None," said Jimmy.

And then she looked at his feet.

"Where are your boots?" she asked in surprise, and Jimmy's jaw dropped. He had
left his boots outside the window of the
Warden's Lodge.

Only for a second did he gape, and then
the humour of the situation overcame him
and he laughed hysterically.

"I wonder if they'll fry bacon after my
funeral?" he said, and Ferdinand looked at
the girl and tapped his forehead significantly.

CHAPTER T.HIRTEEN

THAT morning Tom Elmers had received an urgent summons from his employer.

Elmers had recently come to occupy a dirty little room in a back street of Greenwich, and his landlady found some difficulty in waking him, for Tom Elmers had spent the night before in a. Greenwich bar and the evening had finished with a fight. In his cups Tom Elmers was wont to be boastful about his workmanship, and when he was in that condition he was extremely truculent.

He sat up with a groan, for his head was sore and whizzy, and took the letter from the landlady's hands.

"It came by messenger boy an hour ago, and I've been trying to wake you up ever since, Mr. Elmers."

"All right," growled the young man.

The writing danced before his eyes, but presently he deciphered it and began to dress.

He stopped on his way to the rendezvous, to visit a barber, and for all the heaviness in his eyes and the puffiness of his skin, he was more presentable than Mr. Palythorpe had yet seen him.

"That's better," said that eminent journalist, leaning back in his chair. (The interview took place in Palythorpe's comfortable flat.) "You've been boozing, of course, but you're not so bad as I've seen you. Help yourself to a drink."

Mr. Elmers obeyed.

"And remember that drink has killed more men than earthquakes," said Palythorpe in his best oracular manner. "Have you any news for me?"

Tom shook his head, and was immediately sorry that he had committed so reckless an indiscretion.

"You haven't been to Blake's place again, have you?" asked Palythorpe warningly.

"No, I haven't," was the snarling reply. "You'll get nothing there, I tell you——"

"I know that, now," Mr. Palythorpe interrupted him. "I think I've got the whole story in my two hands. And what's more, I got it by accident."

It was hardly an accident, for in the very heart of the Premier's household was a maid who had been from time to time a very useful informant. She was perhaps the best paid housemaid in London at that period, for Palythorpe could be generous.

"I didn't want to tell you much about this, but unfortunately I must," Palythorpe went on. "I have discovered that Chapelle is spending his nights away from home. Now, that can only mean one thing"; he wagged his fat forefinger solemnly at Tom. "He is leading a double life. I never expected this sort of news for a minute, even in my most optimistic moments, but it only shows that the higher they get the worse they are—it's deplorable," he added virtuously.

"Where does he go?" asked Tom. "Do you want me to find out?"

Mr. Palythorpe's face creased in a smile of amusement.

"I should have to wait a pretty long time before you could find anything out," he

sneered. "No, I know where he goes—I followed him last night in a taxi. He goes to
Blackheath, to a little Government cottage
which is practically inside Greenwich Park.
There is something fishy going on there and
it is your job to find out what?"

"That won't be difficult!" said Tom after
a pause. "If he goes there, I can ask the
servants——"

"You fool!" interrupted the other con-
temptuously. "Do you think, if it was a question of asking servants, that I should employ
a bungler like you to stick your nose inside
the house? Or do you think that the servants
are sitting on the top of the wall waiting to
be questioned? There are no servants, and if
there were, you wouldn't be able to get at
them. The house is supposed to be deserted.
I've made a few enquiries, and there is no
doubt about that. If the Prime Minister
goes there—and, of course, I did not hint to
the fellow who gave me the information that
I dreamt of such a thing—then nobody
guesses as much. What I want you to do,
Tom, is to get inside that place, and it is not
going to be easy. Can you climb?"

It was Mr. Elmers's one accomplishment, that he could climb like a cat, and he stated the fact immodestly.

"That'll be all right," nodded Mr. Palythorpe. "There are some iron spikes on the top of the wall, and you could easily get a rope over them. I want you to get into the grounds and have a good look at the place. If there's a chance of sneaking into the Lodge, and you can stay there any time without anybody knowing you're on the premises, so much the better."

"And what am I to do when I'm there?" asked Tom resentfully. The prospect of spending several days in an empty house did not appeal to him.

"You'll collect anything you can find that'll help me expose Chapelle," said Mr. Palythorpe emphatically; "letters and papers particularly, and if a woman is there, any letters of hers—don't forget, letters are the things I want."

Tom had made a survey of the house in the daylight, a proceeding he relished less than the night visit he had planned. Jimmy Blake lived uncomfortably close to the Lodge, and Jimmy was the last man in the world he wished to meet. That night he waited his opportunity to make an entrance.

He was surprised that there were so many people on the road. He did not know that their destination, too, was the Warden's Lodge, and when he came up to the place, walking (this he did not know) within a few feet of two interested watchers, he was under the impression that the men who had passed him had gone on.

It took him some time to get a grip on the spikes above, but at last his rope caught and held. He had not overstated his claim when he said he could climb like a cat and he was over the wall in less than a minute. His first act when he reached the other side was to unfasten the rope he carried round his waist, which he intended using in case there were other walls to surmount.

He remembered, cursing his carelessness, that he had left the rope he had employed to scale the wall hanging down on the far side and decided to leave the second rope on the ground in readiness for a quick climb.

Very cautiously he pushed through the

bushes and came to the house, as Jimmy had done, near its front entrance. He tried a window, but it was fastened. Then he peered up at the roof. It was too dark to make any attempt that way and he went round to the south side of the house and tried another window. This time he was more successful; the window went up squeakily, and, after waiting to learn if the noise had been heard, he slipped into the room and reached the passage.

He heard a voice and he almost cried out in his astonishment. It was the voice of Joe Sennett! Then there was a movement in a room at the other end of the passage, and Tom Elmers went quickly and noiselessly up the stairs.

The upper part of the house was in darkness. He was on the point of striking a match when he heard a step in the hall below. He groped along the wall and found a door, opened it, and entered the room, closing the door quietly behind him. It was a small room with a flight of steep steps which led to a trap-door in the discoloured ceiling. Tom blew out his match, mounted the steps gin-

gerly and pushed up the trap. It opened, and
he stepped out on to a flat roof, easing down
the heavy wooden cover behind him so that
it made no noise. Here he waited five minutes, his ear pressed to the trap-door, and he
thought he detected the sound of feet, a furtive shuffling sound that ceased suddenly.

Several minutes passed without any further
interruption. They must have gone down to
the lower floor again, he thought, and cautiously raising the trap, he descended into the
cistern room. His foot had hardly touched
the floor when somebody gripped him. For
a second they struggled, and then, hitting out
wildly, Tom dropped his assailant. The
struggle could not have been heard from
below, for when he came out on to the land-
ing, there was no sound. He heard the man
behind him struggling to his feet, and in two
seconds he had reached the hall, had crossed
the room and was through the window into
the grounds.

He ran for the wall where he had left the
rope and flung it up; at the second attempt
the loop caught on the spikes and tightened.

Tom Elmers took one grip of the rope and grinned.

He had been instructed by his employer to devote his whole attention and his every thought to the service which was demanded of him, but in that moment he forgot Mr. Palythorpe and remembered only that somewhere in the darkness an old man whom he hated was searching for him.

"Joe, Joe!" he mocked. "Come out and fight!"

There was a silence, a crash of glass, a running of feet towards him.

He pulled on the rope, but the bar at the top of the wall slipped round and the rope fell at his feet. The running man was nearer, and then out of the darkness leapt a thin pencil of brilliant light, and the silence was broken by the crack of a pistol. . . .

Mr. Palythorpe waited in vain for the return of his lieutenant that night, and finally went to bed.

"He must have got into the house," thought the blackmailer, and with this comforting assurance he went to sleep.

CHAPTER FOURTEEN

"EVERYBODY'S taking this 'Days of Uniting' frightfully seriously. I've had a letter from my governor ordering me to report on the 15th inst."

"Which is the day after to-morrow," said Jimmy.

The other nodded.

"I looked up the calendar, and you're right, Jimmy. According to the governor, people think it's a very good idea."

"Who wouldn't, with free railway travelling chucked in?" said Jimmy in disgust.

Ferdie was practising putts on the garden lawn, and Jimmy was a critical spectator.

The girl came out at that minute with a newspaper in her hand.

"Mr. Blake, have you seen this?" she asked.

"What is it?" asked Jimmy. "Something about the 'Days of Uniting'?"

"No, it is an article in the *Post Herald,* and Stephens says that the police are going round to all the newspaper shops confiscating the paper because of that paragraph."

Jimmy almost snatched the newspaper from Delia's hand. She had marked the place with blue pencil and he read:

MYSTERIOUS ARRESTS

WHAT IS THE NEW GOVERNMENT SCARE?

Three days ago (the paragraph ran) the police, acting on orders from Whitehall, made throughout the country a number of arrests, which can only be described as mysterious. The people who were taken into custody and immediately hurried off to some unknown prison or camp, since they have not been brought up before the magistrates of the districts in which they live, are quite inoffensive, and in some cases, eminent persons whose lives are chiefly distinguished by their absolute blamelessness. Amongst the arrests are those of Professor Mortlake, of Durham University, Sir John Gilgin, the Vicar of Troyston, and scores of other gentlemen who

have no strong political views and who certainly are not criminals. What makes this
occurrence so extraordinary, is the news
which has just come to hand, that the convicts
in Dartmoor Gaol have been all released on
special licence, apparently to make room for
the people who have been arrested in this
wholesale fashion. The release of the Dartmoor convicts is understandable in view of
the Government's fantastic "Days of Uniting." To be consistent, they must extend the
same opportunities for family reunion to the
criminal classes which they extend to those
who are law-abiding citizens. The other arrests are beyond explanation.

"I don't know any of the people who have
been taken," said Jimmy, shaking his head.
"It is rather a rum proceeding."

The afternoon papers carried an authorita-
tive statement issued by the Government, that
the arrests were made for political purposes,
and that the prisoners would be released on
the eve of the 'Days of Uniting' and returned
to their homes in time for the festival.

Jimmy was not interested in this particular

eccentricity of Government; he was too concerned, too worried, by the insoluble mystery which his visit to the Warden's Lodge had set him.

He was in town most of the day, pursuing independent enquiries.

The girl did not know her father was living so close at hand, and he did not enlighten her upon the subject.

No reply had come to his wire to Schaffer, and this puzzled him. A call on one of Gerald's old friends, however, assured him that he had sent the message to the right address.

"I am not quite sure," said the grey-bearded biologist to whom he addressed his enquiry, "but I have a notion that Schaffer is in Switzerland. I read the report of a lecture he delivered there a week ago. He may still be there."

But Jimmy's chief centre of inquisitorial activities was in the House of Commons. Ordinarily he did not take a very great interest in the fluctuation of English politics, and the page in the newspapers containing the Parliamentary reports was one he never

read in any circumstances. But that morning
he had looked up a newspaper file to discover
what other occupation the Premier had than
sweeping floors. The first thing that struck
him was that the answers to questions which
are supposed to be given by the Ministers responsible for the various departments had
been dealt with by Under-Secretaries.

"The Prime Minister hasn't been in the
House for over a week," said a member.
"We're rather sore about it, because not only
he, but Harry Weltman has been absent; and
they did not even turn up the other night to
lead the debate on the new Police Bill. There
is going to be a row, too, about these arrests
and the suppression of the *Post Herald.*"

"Who were the people who were arrested?"
asked Jimmy.

"Oh, small fry," said the member indiffer-
ently. "Somebody was telling me they were
mostly amateur scientists, but of that I have
no information. The release of the criminals
from the gaols is, of course, preposterous."

"Does it extend to the county prisons?"
asked Jimmy.

The member nodded.

"I don't know what the dickens is happening to this country," he said irritably. "For some reason or other Chapelle has made himself a sort of dictator, and has introduced all kinds of regulations without the consent of Parliament. Do you know that foreign newspapers are not admitted into this country?"

Jimmy did not know.

"It is a fact. What is more, there's a tremendously severe censorship on newspaper telegrams. It is almost as though we were at war all over again."

The censorship might have delayed Schaffer's answer, thought Jimmy, as he drove back to Blackheath. What was the meaning of it all? Had the Prime Minister gone mad? And what part was Maggerson playing? Maggerson, the unshaven, foul-looking Maggerson, whom he had seen huddled up over a table in the Warden's Lodge, writing for dear life? And who was the bearded man opposite to him? He was another factor, and the centre of another mystery. He was not a member of the Cabinet. Jimmy had taken the trouble to go to the office of an illustrated newspaper which, he remembered, had published some time before a portrait not only of the Ministers, but of their Under-Secretaries.

The face of the bearded man was not there, and yet he had seen it somewhere. That he was a public man of some sort, Jimmy was certain. He had a queer feeling that if he could discover the identity of the bearded writer, the inexplicable would be made clear.

Delia and Ferdie were out when he got back, and he was unaccountably annoyed. For want of something better to do, he climbed again to the roof and took an observation of the house through the telescope, but this time without adding to his information.

When he came down the two young people were in the hall. Ferdie was hanging up his golf clubs, and Delia was reading a postcard which had come for her.

"Well, any luck, Jimmy?" asked Ferdie.

"None," said Jimmy shortly.

They had rather a cheerless dinner that night. Jimmy was not very talkative, and his gloom affected his friend. Only the girl prevented the meal being spent in absolute silence.

Jimmy was folding his serviette preparatory to rising (he was rapidly acquiring a sense of order), when the door opened, and he jumped to his feet. It was Joe Sennett who stood in the doorway, but a different Joe from the man he had known. His face was puckered and lined, and he looked a very old man indeed.

"I want you, Delia," he said gruffly. "And I'd like to see you, Mr. Blake, after I've seen my girl; or perhaps I'd better see you first."

Delia had run across the room to him with a happy little cry; he took her in his arms, an action which was unlike Joe, who was an undemonstrative man, and she wondered . . .

"Daddy, you aren't ill?" she asked anxiously.

"No, my dear." His voice was rough but tender. "I want to see you alone, darling. Can I come up to your room?"

"You can have the study of Mr. Van Roon's study," said Jimmy.

Joe thought for a moment.

"I'll have your study," he said. "I can get on to the lawn and out of the house from there, can't I?"

Jimmy nodded. He wondered why the girl's father was anxious to leave the Priory by that way.

"Can I see you now, Mr. Blake?"

It was Joe who led the way to the study, and closing the door behind them and without preamble, he began:

"Mr. Blake, what did you see at the Lodge last night?"

"What do you mean?" asked Jimmy steadily.

"What did you see when you were in the grounds of the Lodge last night?"

Jimmy was silent.

"They don't know that it was you yet," Joe went on, "but they'll find out. They sent the boots to London and there are a dozen detectives looking for the owner."

"I saw all there was to be seen," said Jimmy. "What is the explanation, Sennett?"

"There is no explanation that I can give,

sir," said Joe Sennett with a certain dignity.
"Mr. Blake, will you take an old man's advice?"

"What is it, Joe?"

"Get away from Blackheath as quickly as
you can. Take your car and——"

"Bolt?" suggested Jimmy quietly.

"I don't know whether you'd call it bolt-
ing, and I hardly think you'd benefit much if
you did bolt. At any rate, you'd be—" he
stopped himself. "Will you take my advice,
Mr. Blake?"

Jimmy shook his head.

"I shall stay here," he said, "and see it
through, whatever 'it' may be."

Joe nodded.

"I've done all I can for you," he said,
"and now I think I must see Delia."

Jimmy saw his face twitch as though he
was contemplating an unpleasant interview.

"One moment before you go, Sennett."

Jimmy barred the way to the door.

"Is there a logical and reasonable explanation to all this mystery, or is Mr. Chapelle
stark mad?"

"There is a very simple explanation, sir," said Sennett, "but it is not one that I can give, as I told you before."

Jimmy opened the door for him.

"I won't press the question."

"You won't go away either, eh?" said Sennett, looking him straight in the eyes.

"I shall stay here," said Jimmy.

"Very good," said the older man, and without another word walked out of the room, Jimmy following.

Jimmy heard the study door close on Delia and her father, and strolled into the garden. He was there half an hour. When he went back to the study it was empty. He met Mrs. Smith coming downstairs.

"The young lady has gone to her room with a bad headache," she said, "and she did not wish to be disturbed."

"Isn't she coming down again to-night?" asked Jimmy in dismay.

"I don't think so, sir," said the housekeeper, and the young man cursed his luck under his breath.

He went in search of Ferdie and repeated to him the warning which Sennett had given.

"You're in this, Ferdinando," he said, "and I won't disguise from you that there is bad trouble coming to me and possibly to you. Sennett is not the kind of man who would ask us to bolt unless there was serious danger."

"If there's danger to you, there's certainly danger to me," said Ferdie thoughtfully, "and I'll do just as you suggest."

"Well, I advise you to get away," said Jimmy, and Ferdie guffawed loudly.

"Jimmy, you have everything but brains," he said cruelly. "If I bolted, that would bring down suspicion on you. Either we both stay or we both go. And even if it didn't bring suspicion on you, the fact that I had disappeared before your arrest and execution——"

Jimmy made a little face.

"It doesn't sound pretty, does it? But it seems to me a very likely ending to this lark," said Ferdie earnestly. "I was saying—if they came and pinched you and found I had gone, they'd be after me like a shot. Our only chance is to stick together."

He turned to go.

"I say, you don't feel like another visit to the Warden's Lodge to-night?" he suggested.

"No, thank you," said Jimmy fervently. "I have no desire to monkey with a gang which includes a Prime Minister and a Bishop, to say nothing of an eminent scientist."

Ferdie turned back.

"A Prime Minister and a Bishop?" he repeated slowly. "Was the Prime Minister there?"

The last thing in the world Jimmy had intended was to say as much as he had. There was nothing to do now but to tell the whole story.

"I thought you were nutty when you talked about the bacon," said Ferdie after he had finished. "And I still think that you may have been seeing things. But what an unholy combination to butt into—phew! Do you think that Chapelle has gone off his head?"

"No, and I don't think the Bishop has either," said Jimmy. "I should say the Bishop of Fleet was too shrewd and tough a man to be led into an adventure of this kind by an obvious lunatic. Ferdie, you were boasting the other day that you had a couple of Mills Bombs. Take your car and go up to your flat and get them, like a good fellow."

"Why?" asked the astonished Ferdie. "Are you thinking of bombing the old boy?"

"I did have some such idea," said Jimmy dryly.

"When shall I go?"

"Go now."

And Ferdie went off to get his noisy car.

An hour later the study bell rang and Stephens answered it.

"Bring Mrs. Smith here," said Jimmy, looking up from his writing-table. "I want you to witness my will."

"Your will, sir?" said Stephens, startled.

"Hurry," said Jimmy. "I have followed the example of Lord Harry and have left five years' salary to everybody in my employ, and if you don't stop looking like an asphyxiated cod-fish, you won't benefit."

It was his will that he had written, a somewhat voluminous document, and his two servants, fluttered and apprehensive, affixed their signatures as witnesses. Also Jimmy had destroyed all his private correspondence and made a rough survey of his financial position. He told himself that he was wasting time and acting like a scare-cat, but he had realized that in the event of his sudden demise his property would go to the State, and just then he had a grudge against the State.

Neither Mrs. Smith nor Stephens read the provisions of the will, so they were not aware that the principal beneficiary was a girl who at that moment was sitting in her locked room, her hands clasped on her lap, staring out into the night with eyes that were big and tragic and hopeless.

Jimmy had given up any hope of seeing Delia that night, when he heard the door of the study open and close again.

"I didn't ring for the coffee, but you can put it there," he said without raising his eyes from the letter he was writing.

There was no response and no movement, and then he looked up.

It was Delia. Her face, at any time, showed little colour, but now it was a dead white, and her eyes seemed to have grown darker, so that by contrast with her pallor they looked black.

"Delia!"

He went towards her, his hands outstretched, and she took them in hers, and all the time her eyes were fixed on his. He saw in them fear and appeal—The Terror had come to her and had frozen her stiff and speechless.

"Delia!" He whispered the word and, taking her by the arms, shook her gently.

He saw her pale lips flutter and tremble as she tried to speak.

"For God's sake, Delia . . . what is wrong?"

And then she spoke. Her voice was faint and shaky, but it became more steady as she went on.

"Jimmy! Do you . . . do you love me?"

He nodded. He could not have spoken.

"You meant . . . all you said in the garden . . . that night?"

"Every word," his voice seemed that of a stranger, it was so cracked and strained.

"Will you marry me . . . at once . . . tomorrow? Please, please!"

He put his arms about her and drew her tighter and tighter to him, and the fear in her eyes died and the old soft woman-look returned . . . the old shining Delia look, only more glorious by the love and faith and surrender in them.

"My dear!"

He muttered the words, his lips to hers.

Something wonderful had happened . . . how? why? he did not know nor care. He was shaking, his arms were weak and trembling and his knees were feeble . . . it seemed as if the strength of life had been sapped in this joy.

"You'll do it to-morrow . . . you can get a special license, can't you? You will, please . . . please, Jimmy dear!"

She was crying and laughing.

"I never thought I'd be happy again," she breathed. "I know now that all my . . . fine plans . . . were stupid and unreal . . . but this is real, isn't it, Jimmy? It's the essence, the essence of life . . ."

It was she who raised her face and kissed him, holding her lips to his, her arm clasped about his neck, her eyes, divinely beautiful and lit with a new fire, so close to his that he felt the flick of eyelashes against his.

"Delia . . . wonderful!" he gulped the words and felt big and coarse and clumsy as he led her to the couch . . . "what magic has been working, darling? I never dreamt of this happiness."

"It's the magic of . . . of . . ."

For a second the wild terror he had seen smouldered in her dark eyes and then she broke into a passion of weeping.

"To-morrow . . . to-morrow . . . please, please!" she sobbed, and Jimmy held her in his arms and comforted her.

She smiled through tears, checked a sob and murmured:

" 'As a mother comforteth her child so will I comfort you.' "

And then she became suddenly quiet and he thought she had swooned, but she was sleeping peacefully. He held her motionless as the hours passed, and then his head began to nod and he, too, slept.

It was Ferdinand Ponter who found them so. He came in at midnight, his coat-pockets bulging, and stopped at the sight; then he stepped softly from the room and closed the door behind him.

"Well, I'm blowed!" said Ferdinand, and shook his head. "Wrong, quite wrong," he muttered as he walked up the stairs to his room, "especially if they're not engaged!"

CHAPTER FIFTEEN

JIMMY went early to the office of the registrar of the district to give notice of his marriage.

"Is it possible for the ceremony to be performed to-morrow?" he asked.

That morning he had read up the regulations dealing with the time of special licences and had made the unhappy discovery that one clear day must elapse between the "notice" and the ceremony. But he had a dim recollection that during the war special facilities were given, and these might still be obtainable.

"You can be married to-day," was the surprising answer.

"To-day?" repeated Jimmy, delighted.

"Yes. The Chief Registrar sent us a memorandum yesterday to that effect. The Government and the Archbishop have issued

a schedule to the Proclamation giving special
facilities for people who want to be married
before 'The Days of Uniting.' "

Before he had finished the delighted Jimmy
had gripped him by the hand.

"My lad," he said, "you're an angel!"

"His lad" was thirty, dyspeptic and wore
glasses. Jimmy supplied all the information
necessary for the issue of the licence. He
guessed at the girl's age, and took it for
granted that she had no other name than
Delia; and then he drove into Greenwich,
stopped before a jeweller's shop, guessed
again at the size of her finger, and was at the
Priory with the ring in his pocket before
Delia knew he had left the house.

Ferdie and Stephens were the witnesses,
and the ceremony was ridiculously short and
simple; fifty words spoken by each, and they
were man and wife!

"I shouldn't have believed it was so jolly
easy, Jimmy," said Ferdie, poising a pen in
his hand over the register. "This is a bit of a
warning to boys, isn't it? And it takes twelve
months to get a divorce! A fellow might be
yanked into a place like this, and go out with

a perfectly strange wife, before the poor boy knew what was happening to him."

Beyond the words she had repeated after the registrar, Delia had not spoken. Some of her colour had come back and her face wore that ethereal, exalted look which Jimmy had seen before. Once she looked at the ring on her finger and smiled, but she made no other sign till the last entry had been made and the registrar had handed to her the marriage certificate in a tiny envelope, and then she said:

"I am very glad."

She slipped her arm through Jimmy's, and they went out of the dull office together, to meet the unmistakable detectives who were standing before the door.

"Mr. Blake?" said one of these.

"My name is Blake," said Jimmy.

He felt the hand of the girl grip tighter on his arm.

"I am Inspector Cartwright, and I hold a warrant for your arrest."

"On what charge?" asked Jimmy quietly.

"Treason-felony," was the reply, and Jimmy nodded.

"I wondered what it would be," he said.
He gently disengaged Delia's hand.

"You had better go with Ferdie, dear," he
said; and she did not speak, but slowly drew
her arm from his, looking at him in a dazed
hurt way that broke his heart to see.

A taxi-cab was waiting. He was hustled
in by the police officers and in a few minutes
was out of sight.

"I don't understand," the girl said slowly,
and then collapsed in Ferdie's arms.

The cab drove into the yard of Blackheath
Road Police Station. Jimmy noticed that his
captors did not go through the formality of
charging him, but led him straight away to
a cell which had evidently been prepared, for
on the rough wooden bench which served
prisoners for a bed, a mattress had been
placed.

Left alone, Jimmy sat down with his head
in his hands, to consider the position. He did
not doubt that he was in the greatest danger.
The Prime Minister was under the impression that he had surprised a State secret, and
the fate which, for some reason, had overtaken Gerald Van Roon would also be his.

Or were they sending him to join the thousand or so harmless citizens who had been arrested in the previous week? Certainly no charge was preferred, and no attempt was made to question him.

His lunch was brought, and at half-past five a substantial tea was carried into the cell by the jailer. He must have received instructions not to converse with the prisoner, for he made no answer to Jimmy's questions.

The day had passed like an eternity. He tried to sleep, but the moment his head touched the pillow, his mind went to Delia, and it was all thought of her that he was striving so desperately to keep from his mind.

At nine o'clock the lock snapped back, the cell door opened, and the jailer came in.

"Put out your hands," he said curtly; and Jimmy obeyed.

A pair of handcuffs were snapped on his wrists. Taking his arm, the jailer led him along the corridor into the yard. A closed car was waiting, and beside the open door was a tall man, whose face was in the shadow. Jimmy stepped into the car and sank back with a sigh of comfort upon the luxurious upholstery.   The stranger entered after him, slammed the door, and the car moved off.

Jimmy knew where he was being taken, long before the machine had stopped at the green postern gate.

Although it was much earlier in the evening than the people of Warden's Lodge came and went, the road was deserted, and only one person saw his entry.   Delia, lying flat on the grass, had kept watch since nightfall, and now her vigil was rewarded.

Jimmy was pushed through the door, and hurried along the path he had trodden the night before; but this time he entered by the front door.

The man who was with him stood revealed in the light of the lamp which hung on the wall of the room into which he was pushed.

"Well, Mr. Blake," said Lord Harry pleasantly.   "We are very sorry to put you to this inconvenience, but if you know as much about our business as we fear you do, you will quite understand why it is impossible to leave you at large."

Jimmy made no reply, and Lord Harry Weltman, stripping off his coat, opened a cigarette case and offered it to Jimmy. The young man extracted a cigarette with his manacled hands, and the Minister of Defence lit it for him.

"You can sit down," he said courteously; and as Jimmy accepted the invitation, he went on. "You were in the grounds the night before last, of course. Were you alone?"

"Quite alone," said Jimmy.

"Did anybody know that you were coming?"

"Nobody," replied Jimmy promptly.

"You had no companion at all?"

"No, sir."

"Not even your friend, Mr. Ponter?"

"He was at the Priory and had no idea I was coming," lied Jimmy.

"How did you get over the wall without assistance?"

"I brought a collapsible ladder in my car." Jimmy could tell the truth here, and he saw that Lord Harry was impressed.

"Now, Mr. Blake, I think we had better understand one another; and I might tell you at first that I am charged with the part of extracting from you the fullest possible details of your knowledge. What did you see when you were in the grounds?"

"I saw you burying the man Elmers," said Jimmy.

"Elmers?"

Lord Harry stared at the other and then went on:

"You imagined you did," he said. "And then?"

"I looked through the window and I saw the Prime Minister sweeping up the room, and the Bishop frying something, I think it was bacon, in a frying-pan."

"It was bacon," agreed the other gravely, "and it was very excellent bacon. What else did you see?"

"I saw Mr. Maggerson and a gentleman whose name I do not know, sitting at a table writing."

"Do you know who the other man was?" asked Lord Harry quickly.

"I haven't the slightest idea, my Lord," said Jimmy, and met the cold scrutiny of the Minister's eye without quailing.

"Were you near enough to see what they were writing?"

Jimmy shook his head.

"And you say on your honour you do not know who the other man was?"

"No, sir, I do not."

"Well, I can give you a little information on that subject, but whether you will learn or not depends entirely on the view the Prime Minister takes of your case."

Jimmy's heart beat a little faster. He could not misunderstand the significance of that last remark. If they adjudged him to die, he would be let into their secret. If they exonerated him from antagonism, or whatever it was they feared, he would remain in ignorance.

He raised his shackled hands to take the cigarette from his lips, and Lord Harry, noticing the gesture, smiled.

"I'm sorry we can't release you from those fetters," he said. "I do sincerely hope you can convince us that you're not—dangerous."

"In what way dangerous?" asked Jimmy.

"The only form of dangerousness we recognise is an inclination to talk," said Lord Harry, and went out of the room.

He was gone a quarter of an hour, and

came back with the Prime Minister. Mr.
Chapelle had changed considerably since
Jimmy had seen him last. He had passed
from the pleasantly old to the painfully old,
but he was as straight and held his head as
high as ever, and when he spoke there was no
break in his rasping, menacing tone.

"You would not keep out of this, Mr.
Blake, and you have yourself to thank for
your serious position. I was afraid you
would. Your cousin could have saved his
life. I doubt very much whether you can."

He looked at the floor, fingering his chin.

"Bring him into the room," he said; and,
at a nod from Lord Harry, Jimmy followed
him into the apartment at the back of the
house, that very room into which he had
peered.

The big table which he had then seen had
gone, and so, too, had the bearded man and
Maggerson. Old Sennett stood with his
back to the fire, his hands behind him, but
he did not meet Jimmy's eyes. Only the
Bishop, suave, pleasant, almost jocular in his
greeting, seemed to be free from a kind of

strained nervousness which affected them all, save he.

"This is a bad business, Mr. Blake," he said, "a very bad business. And you were married to-day, I hear?"

Jimmy looked at Joe Sennett. The old man did not raise his eyes.

"Yes, I was married to-day," said Jimmy quietly. "In fact, about four minutes before your police gentlemen abducted me."

"What are we to do about this man?" asked the Prime Minister impatiently. "I am not prepared to keep him here."

"What are you prepared to do?" said Jimmy. He was recovering a little of his balance.

"I am prepared to order your destruction," said Chapelle coldly. "I shall not hesitate at that, believe me! My mind is divided on the question of expediency. I would not kill a fly unnecessarily," he added in a lower voice, "and all that is human in me will deplore your death, Mr. Blake, bitterly, bitterly!"

Jimmy could not restain a grin.

"It will be worth something to know that I am sincerely mourned by so eminent a man as yourself, sir," he said; "and I shall naturally do my best to save you this unnecessary sorrow."

"Lord Harry tells me that you did not know the other gentleman who was here."

Jimmy shook his head.

"No, sir."

"You're sure of that?"

The Prime Minister eyed him keenly.

"I am prepared to swear to that, sir; I don't know him, although I seem to have seen his portrait in an illustrated paper." He knitted his brows. "Why, of course, it is the Astronomer Royal, Sir John Dart!"

Before the words were out he bitterly regretted his indiscretion. He saw the Prime Minister's chest heave up and heard the long-drawn sigh.

"I was afraid you would," said the Premier in a low voice.

All the time Joe Sennett had said no word, nor had he so much as looked at the prisoner. Now, however, he raised his eyes, and they

met Jimmy's for the space of a second, and
then dropped again.

"I was desperately afraid you would," the
Prime Minister was saying. "Well—" he
looked at Lord Harry, and the tall, hard-
faced man nodded. "You don't think," the
Prime Minister hesitated, "that if we kept
him prisoner——"

"The longer he has to think, the more he
will understand," said Lord Harry significantly. "If this was the 15th instead of the
14th I would say 'No,' but we cannot afford
to keep him alive."

"I agree."

The Premier nodded.

Jimmy's heart went cold and he was seized
with a momentary trembling, then he grew
cool. As he pulled himself erect to face the
ordeal, he saw Lord Harry's hand go to his
pocket and come out holding a pistol.

Joe had turned so that he faced the fire.
The Prime Minister had his hand on the
handle of the door preparatory to leaving the
room, and from where he stood Jimmy could
not see the Bishop.

Then a cold rage seized him. Why should
he die? ·He was innocent of any wrong-
doing.

The pistol rose slowly until it covered him,
and then Jimmy spoke.

" 'I would not kill thine unprepared
spirit,' " quoth he sneeringly. "Really, gentlemen, you are barbarians, and you have a
Bishop on the premises, too."

Lord Harry dropped his pistol.

"What do you want?" he asked.

"I want an hour," said Jimmy.

Lord Harry shook his head.

The Prime Minister turned at the sound of
Jimmy's voice.

"Give him five minutes," he said.

There was just a faint hope in Jimmy's
heart. Had anybody seen him being brought
in? Had Ferdie guessed where he would be
taken? If any attempt was made——

"Crash!"

The window splintered into fragments.
Somebody had shattered it with an iron bar,
and that somebody, Jimmy knew, was Ferdie
Ponter.

"Quick, Jimmy!" yelled a voice.

He dashed to the window, held up his chained hands, and something round and egg-shaped was thrush into them. Stooping he drew out the pin of the Mills Bomb with his teeth.

"Shoot, gentlemen," he mocked. "But as sure as you do, this bomb will fall from my hands and explode. If you come near me," he said, as the Minister made a movement, "it will also fall, and your precious secret will be a secret no more."

There was a silence, broken only by the painful breathing of the Bishop.

"Take off his handcuffs," said the Prime Minister at last. "I will give you my word of honour, Mr. Blake, that you shall not be harmed. Bring in your friend from outside."

Jimmy hesitated, then walked to the window.

"You can come in, Ferdie. Are you alone?"

There was no reply to this, and then the door was opened.

Ferdie came in, and following him came Delia. She took no notice of anybody else, but, walking across the room, she took Jimmy's hand in hers.

The two Ministers had left the room. Joe still stared gloomily at the floor, and had taken no notice of his daughter. The only stranger was the Bishop, who had dropped into the chair by the fire, his chin sunk on his breast.

"I saw them take you in," she said in a low voice. "I went straight back to Ferdie. He was wonderful, Jimmy. He remembered the bombs he had brought back for you, and we came straight across. He didn't want me to come, but I just had to." She smiled. "There's a telegram for you, I found it on the hall-stand just as I was leaving the house."

Jimmy slipped the buff envelope into his pocket.

"And what next?" he asked.

She shook her head.

"Father, what next?" she repeated.

He threw out his hands in a gesture of despair.

"How do I know, my dear? Have you told Mr. Blake——"

She shook her head.

"Told me what?" asked Jimmy quickly.

"Perhaps you will know."

The door opened and the Prime Minister came back; this time he was accompanied by the two men whom Jimmy had seen before —Maggerson and the stranger, the Astronomer Royal.

"Blake," said the Prime Minister without preliminary, "I am going to tell you the strangest story that any man has ever told, or ever heard, and that story will explain why your cousin met his death at my hands."

"At your hands?" gasped Jimmy, doubting his senses.

The Prime Minister nodded.

"By accident I executed Gerald Van Roon in the cause of humanity," he said solemnly, "not because he was a bad man, for I know nothing of him that was not creditable and, indeed, noble. But because he was an indiscreet man. He died for his principles."

CHAPTER SIXTEEN

"MR. MAGGERSON"—began the Prime Minister—"is a very old friend of mine. We were at school together, and our early lives ran upon parallel lines. Maggerson is, I need hardly tell you, a brilliant man of science. I myself am a dabbler in science. I am passionately fond of mathematics and physics, and, by a remarkable coincidence, two other members of the Cabinet were also men who had leanings that way. For years we made a point of dining every Thursday night, a practice which was discontinued after I accepted the leadership of my party.

"At these gatherings, my friend, the Lord Bishop of Fleet, was generally present, though he was not Bishop in those days, but the headmaster of a school, as Mr. Ponter probably knows.

"I tell you this much, because I feel that it is well that you should know my authority for acting as I have done, and because, by reason of those friendships, I have been able to call upon three of the cleverest mathematicians in Great Britain to confirm a certain discovery which we made, or rather which Mr. Maggerson made, a little more than a week ago. Mr. Maggerson is—and of this you must also be aware—the inventor of a new calculus, or rather a Table of Variations which is used by mathematicians and those who have relations with the exact sciences all over the world.

"I think that this story really starts," the Prime Minister went on, "on the day of the luncheon party which I gave, partly to celebrate his return from America and partly to celebrate the issue of his amended calculus, four hundred thousand copies of which were, I believe, sold within a week of issue.

"As you know, Mr. Maggerson did not arrive, and when he did he was in a condition bordering upon—hysteria, I can think of no better word. It took us some time before we could get him calm, and when we did it was to learn something which I think stunned every one of us. Fortunately, there were only us five friends present. My secretary was away in Glasgow in connection with a meeting which I was to address. Besides myself and Maggerson, there were Lord Harry Weltman, Mr. Stope-Kendrick and the Bishop in the room.

"It is rather difficult to explain to a layman, one who is apparently not interested in mathematics, the exact functions of the Table of Variations with which the name of Maggerson is associated. By its use it is possible to make the most exact, indeed, the only exact, astronomical calculations that can be made. Those calculations, as you probably know, if worked out without the aid of what, for a better term, I will call a mathematical ready-reckoner, would take years to accomplish, and it was with the object of measuring the immeasurable, that Newton and Leibnitz produced their calculi.

"On the day before the luncheon Mr. Maggerson read a note in one of the foreign papers concerning the discovery of a comet which interested him. In the afternoon he visited Greenwich and had lunch with the Astronomer Royal. They discussed the appearance of the comet in the northern skies, a comet which was neither Enekes, which had been sighted the year before, nor Winneckes, and which was either a new-comer in the heavens or else the identical comet on which Newton based his famous calculations. This, however, they decided it could not be, for Newton's comet was not due for another hundred and fifteen years. Now, hitherto, in calculating the periodicity of comets, there had been considerable difficulties in making accurate predictions, difficulties due to the influences exercised by various planets, which attract the wanderer from its course. Jupiter in particular seems to have an extraordinary influence upon the cometary matter.

"By means of Maggerson's table, however, the most extraordinary accurate results can be obtained, and after taking the longitude of the perihelion, etc., Maggerson went home and began to work out the character and the identity of the comet.

"Then, gentlemen"—the voice of the Prime Minister was lowered—"he made an astonishing discovery. It was this, *that on the 16th of May of this year, the comet 'X,' for no name has been given to this wanderer, must inevitably collide with the earth!"*

For a second Jimmy's heart stopped beating.

"Inevitably?" he repeated.

The Prime Minister nodded.

"The character of a comet is not known. You can only take the spectrum and discover that it contains certain hydrocarbons, sodium and other chemical constituents; but whether the nucleus, which is bigger than the earth, is solid, or whether it is as vaporous as its attenuated tail, nobody knows. If it is solid" —he paused—"if it is solid and the collision occurs, it is certain that human life, or, for the matter of that, any life, cannot exist on the earth."

Jimmy cleared his throat.

"You mean, sir, that on the 16th all civilization, all that the world is and means for us, may be wiped away?" His voice sank to a whisper.

The Premier nodded.

"Maggerson was not satisfied with his work. He began again, and working all night, he arrived at a similar result; and then it was, and forgetting he was not dressed, forgetting everything except the approaching cataclysm, and the terror into which the world would fall, if the news were known, he ran from his house, and did not stop running until he reached Number 10 Downing Street."

One of the men in the room had a loud watch. Jimmy heard it distinctly.

"Then what happened?" he found voice to ask.

"Maggerson asked me and Stope-Kendrick to check his calculations. In conjunction with the Astronomer Royal we worked carefully throughout the next night, and a portion of the next day. We were beginning to attract attention. The newspaper reporters had noted that we were together, practically locked in one room; and then it was that I thought of the Warden's Lodge. It was Crown property and had been standing empty for many years: It was near to London, but, what was more important, it was within a few minutes' walk of the Royal Observatory.

"It was after we had installed ourselves that the Astronomer Royal suggested we should send for Gerald Van Roon. This course was heartily approved both by Maggerson and by myself, though you, Lord Harry, objected. I can only wish most fervently," said the Prime Minister, "that we had listened to your objections. Lord Harry pointed out that Gerald was a man of extremely high principles, and that he had very definite views on the duty of science to the public. We had some trouble with him last year when he was called into consultation over the failure of the wheat and corn crop."

Jimmy nodded.

"I remember; he was writing an article on that very subject on the night of his death," he said.

"However," continued the Prime Minister, "we overcame Lord Harry's objections, and Harry and Stope-Kendrick themselves went across to your house and delivered the message, returning with Gerald Van Roon. In the meantime the Bishop had gone to arouse the Government printer, Mr. Sennett here, whom you know. We felt, as a preliminary measure, that it was necessary to warn military authorities that some sort of trouble might be expected. What we most feared was the news leaking out that such a collision was inevitable. The destruction of the earth, the wiping off of life, will be a matter so terrifically sudden that nobody will realize what has happened. There is no terror in death—swift, painless, universal"—he said quietly; "but there is a terror of fear which would drive men and women frantic, which would reduce the world to a shrieking madhouse. Mr. Van Roon came. We told him quickly the facts as we knew them, namely, that on the 16th of May, the unknown comet would cross the orbit of the earth at a point where a collision was impossible to avoid.

"At first he was horrified, and then he sat down to study the tables which Maggerson and the Bishop had prepared between them. When he had finished there happened what Lord Harry had feared. Your cousin was a deeply religious man, and he insisted that the world should know. That was, naturally, a course which we determined should not be taken. There was an angry scene; the end of it was, Gerald Van Roon walked through that very door with the words:

" 'Whatever you may say, Prime Minister, I consider it my duty to communicate to the world the danger which threatens our existence.'

"And there was no doubt whatever that he intended to put his threat into execution. For the moment we were paralysed, and not until he had left the house did it come to me just what his action would mean.

"We had made some rough preparations, crude and unskillful, to deal with any intrusion into our sanctuary. I had brought down an automatic pistol which my son gave me after the war, and this was then lying on the mantelpiece. I snatched it up and ran after your cousin. He was half-way across the garden. It was raining heavily, I remember, because I slipped on the greasy grass, and in slipping I fired. I don't think I had any intention of killing him; my plan was to bring him back and hold him a prisoner, but as I slipped I must have thrown out my hand and gripped at the trigger. I am not used to the ways of automatic pistols, and I did not realize that so long as the trigger is pressed the weapon continues to fire. I heard five shots and could not realize that it was I who had fired them, until I saw Gerald Van Roon lying senseless on the grass.

"I came back to the house, and we had a consultation. The position was a dreadful one. To explain his death would mean to explain the circumstances under which he met his death. There was nothing to do but to carry out Lord Harry's suggestion, which was that he should be carried on to the Heath and left there.

"I was perfectly certain at the time that he was dead, for he showed no signs of life, and the wounds"—the Premier shivered—"were terrible! We carried him out just before daybreak and left him, and his fate you know. I might say that Mr. Sennett was not present; indeed, Mr. Sennett did not come into our confidence until a few days ago, when it became necessary to prepare our proclamation."

"The object of the Proclamation being to unite families for the final day of life?"

The Prime Minister nodded.

"It was the last service which we could render to humanity," he said, "and that will

also explain to you, Mr. Blake, the release of
the convicts from the various prisons throughout the country."

"It does not explain the arrest of thousands
of innocent men," said Jimmy.

A faint smile played at the corners of the
Premier's delicate mouth.

"Those innocent men were all gentlemen
who possessed telescopes," he said. "They
were, in fact, corresponding members of
various astronomical societies, and it was very
necessary that we should not allow them to
make independent calculations. There is one
more matter to explain, and that is—the end
of poor Kendrick." The Premier's voice
shook. "He was my very dearest friend,"
he said, "a quiet scholarly man on whose
mind the knowledge of this terrible danger
produced a deplorable effect. We had met
earlier one evening, and the Bishop remarked
upon the strange appearance of the poor
fellow. We missed him for a moment—and
in that moment he had passed through the
gate . . . I don't want to think about it."

Jimmy looked round the room from face to
face. The girl's eyes had not left his; her lips

were set tight. As to Ferdie, he was all blank amazement.

"Perhaps you would like to see—our friend," said the Prime Minister.

Jimmy wondered whom he was talking about.

"He is very clearly visible to-night," Mr. Chapelle went on; and Jimmy knew that he was talking of the comet. "But I am afraid he will not impress you."

"I did not know there was a comet visible," said Jimmy.

"Very few people do," said the Prime Minister, "although one or two indiscreet references appeared in the newspapers, emanating from foreign correspondents; that is why we established the press censorship. It is a curious comet, because it has little or no tail, and that is probably why it has escaped general observation."

He led the way to the dark garden, and it was the Astronomer Royal who directed Jimmy's eyes to the north-western firmament. Presently he saw it! A blurred spot of light like a star seen through a thin cloud.

"He doesn't look very formidable, does

he?" said the Prime Minister as he led the way back to the room, "and yet, Mr. Blake, he is the world's terror. For billions of years we have escaped contact with any of these waifs of space, and there are thousands of great men who are emphatic that the laws which govern the movement of celestial bodies make it absolutely impossible that contact can be made."

"There is only one thing I would like to ask you, sir," said Jimmy, "although I realize that I have no right whatever to question you."

"You may ask anything you wish," interrupted Mr. Chapelle.

"There was no accident in your shooting the man who came into your garden the other night, the night I left my boots under your window?"

It was Lord Harry who replied.

"I killed him," he said simply; "he was a local criminal named Day, a poor devil who specializes in stealing lead-piping."

"Day?" said Jimmy, staring at him.

Lord Harry nodded.

"We thought we heard suspicious sounds,

and I went into the garden and I found him sliding down a water-pipe with a coil of lead pipe which he had taken from a disused cistern. Not knowing who he was, or what was his object, I called on him to stand. He ran, and I shot him."

Jimmy collapsed into a chair.

"Then it was not Tom Elmers!" he said hollowly.

"Tom Elmers?" It was Joe who spoke. "Was he here?" and Jimmy told him all he had seen on the night he broke into the grounds.

"That is serious," said the Prime Minister. "Do you know him, Mr. Sennett?"

"I know him," replied Joe, startled; "he is dangerous, sir—he would probably understand every calculation that has been made in this house. I should say that next to myself he is the finest mathematical printer in England."

"You did not see him again after he disappeared over the wall?" said Chapelle, turning to Jimmy.

Jimmy shook his head.

"No, I didn't see him. I was perfectly

satisfied that he was the gentleman you were burying."

"That's very, very bad," said the Prime Minister. "Is he an enemy of yours?"

"Not of mine, sir."

"He is of mine," said Joe. "He wished to marry my daughter, and neither she nor I wanted anything to do with him, and he took to drink. My own impression is that he is a little mad. He always was a violent, undisciplined man."

There was a long silence, broken by the Prime Minister.

"That man must be found," he said quietly. "He may be concealed in this very house. You have seen or heard nothing, Maggerson?"

The great Maggerson shook his head. Apparently, he was the only one who spent the whole of his time at the Warden's Lodge.

"We had better make a search," said Lord Harry, shortly. "You and your friend come along, Mr. Blake."

Jimmy followed him into the broad panelled hall and up the rickety stairs. Ferdie brought up the rear, carrying an oil lamp.

The gloomy rooms were empty and in a sad state of disrepair. Only one, where Maggerson had slept and in which Jimmy had seen him through his telescope, was occupied. There were five rooms on the upper floor, and each room was explored without producing any other sign of life than mice.

"He's not here," said Jimmy. "Are there any cellars?"

"None," replied Lord Harry. "The only place on which he could conceal himself is the roof, which is flat, like most of the houses in this neighborhood."

He pointed to a trap-door leading from a small cistern room. It was reached by a steep ladder.

"The last man who was in here," began Lord Harry as he climbed the steps, "was the unfortunate burglar whom you saw being buried. There," he pointed, "is the end of the piping he stole."

He pushed up the trap, and Jimmy followed him into the night. It was both impossible and inexpedient to bring up the lamp, said Ferdie; and they had to conduct their search in the darkness. They were groping their way along the parapet, when they heard a crash behind them. It was the trap-door falling. Immediately afterwards came a yell below and a smashing of glass. Jimmy stumbled across the roof, found the trap and flung it up. From below came the smell of kerosene, but the lamp had gone and so also had Ferdie. Jimmy dropped to the floor and ran downstairs. The front door was open, and he flew out into the night. He saw a figure in the half-darkness and then heard Ferdinand's voice.

"Sorry, old man; he climbed the wall and I haven't the key of the gate."

"Did you see him?"

"No, but I felt him," said Ferdie, grimly.

When he came into the light they saw he had a long cut on his cheek.

"Lost him," he said laconically.

He had not seen the "him." Standing at the foot of the ladder beneath the trap-door, the man had suddenly dropped on him; the light had been extinguished, and before he could pull himself to his feet, the attacker was half-way down the stairs.

CHAPTER SEVENTEEN

THE Prime Minister turned to Maggerson.

"You wrote a summary of your observations. Those are the only papers he could get at—it would take too long to follow the calculations," he said. "Will you bring the summary down. It will also help Mr. Blake to understand. I fear I may have failed to impress upon you the seriousness of our discovery."

"I think I understand fairly well, sir," said Jimmy quietly, after Maggerson had gone upstairs to his room. "On the sixteenth, at some hour——"

"At half-past four in the afternoon by Greenwich mean-time," said the Prime Minister. "The point of contact will in all probability be within a hundred miles of the South Pole, but the effect will be just as disastrous as if it struck the city of London."

Jimmy nodded.

"At that hour, sir, you expect the world to be destroyed?"

"Not destroyed," corrected the Prime Minister. "I think the world will go on rolling through space; it will probably stagger, perhaps for a few seconds."

"And it will require no more than that," asked Jimmy in amazement, "to wipe off all form of life?"

"Some life may still exist," said the Prime Minister. "For example, we expect that fish —especially the deep-sea fish—and a very large proportion of the others, will still continue living. Certain insects, too, will continue; and it is possible, though very improbable, that mammalian and even human life will be left with a representative or two. It depends entirely on the effect which the impact may have upon the atmosphere. The atmospheric belt may be burnt up, leaving the world a cold cinder, in which case, of course, even the lowest form of sea life would perish."

Maggerson came in at that moment, a worried frown on his face.

"Did you take the summary from my room, Chapelle?" he asked.

"No," said the Prime Minister quickly. "Has it gone?"

"I had it under my pillow. I swear I put it there last night, but it's not there now."

Jimmy, still dazed and almost crushed by the news he had heard, could only wonder that such a minor matter as the disappearance of a summary, whatever that might be, should affect the Prime Minister so.

"We must get that man," he said.

"What use would the summary be to him?" asked Lord Harry. "And who would publish it, supposing he took it to an editor?"

"I know a man who would publish it," said the Prime Minister between his teeth. "Though it may seem a fantastic theory on my part, I believe Elmers was sent by him to discover what is going on at the Warden's Lodge."

Jimmy, with Delia and Ferinand Ponter, left the dark house by the postern gate he had come to know so well. They walked across the Heath, each in his or her own way reflecting on what the days would bring forth.

In silence they turned into the dining-room; and Stephens, who was sitting at the dining-room table, his head upon his hands, jumped up as if he had seen a ghost.

"Mr. Blake, sir," he stammered. He was speechless until he found the formula which came readiest: "Can I get anything?"

He was eager and trembling, and Jimmy shook his head with a smile.

"No, thank you, Stephens," he said.

But there was one who was not to be denied.

"Beer, Stephens, my lad," he said; "nut-brown ale—and draw it with a froth."

"Beer!" said Jimmy, with a wry little smile. "I can't understand you, Ferdie; you're a weird bird! I suppose you don't realize the significance of all the Prime Minister told us."

"I only realize that I want beer in large quantities," said Ferdie firmly. "It's rather a pity this sort of thing's going to happen. It's a jolly old world when you come to think of it." And Jimmy shuddered.

"Your good health, Mrs. Blake."

He raised his tankard, and Jimmy looked up and stared open-mouthed at him.

"Mrs. Blake?" he repeated. "Who the dickens—" and then he looked at the girl, her mouth twitching with laughter. "Good Lord, I'm married!" he gasped. He had forgotten the fact.

Joe Sennett came across from the Warden's Lodge the next morning and brought the lastest news.

"Half the police force of England are searching for that fellow," he said, shaking his head. "He's a thoroughly bad lot. I suppose Delia told you she knew, Mr. Blake?"

"About—" Jimmy hesitated.

"I broke faith with Mr. Chapelle in telling my daughter, but I was certain she would not tell even you." The old man bit his lips. "I wonder—" and then: "Have you any friends or relations with whom you are spending to-morrow?" he asked.

"No, Joe," said Jimmy quietly, "except my wife and, I hope, my father-in-law. I intend leaving this house to-morrow morning early in my car and taking Delia and you with me. The servants I am sending to their homes. Mr. Ponter is going to his father's house."

"Where do you intend going, Mr. Blake?"

"To Salisbury Plain," said Jimmy. "I

want the openness of it, and Delia agrees. I want to be away from houses, and the sight of humanity suffering, if it does suffer—please God it will not."

"At what hour, sir?"

"At daybreak," said Jimmy, and his father-in-law went up to his room without further comment.

His work was done, Jimmy learnt later. The country was quiet; no word of the approaching catastrophe had been spoken and the necessity for secret orders, printed or otherwise, had passed. Every railway was running to the utmost limit of its rolling-stock, carrying, for the first time in its history, passengers who paid no fare and who were stopped at no barriers.

Jimmy drove up to town that morning to make sure that the servants at his flat were taking their holiday.

As he drove down Blackheath Hill that bright May morning, with the sky a fleckless blue and the world bathed in yellow sunshine, it seemed impossible that this terrible thing could happen. Women were shopping in a busy thoroughfare through which he passed;

laden trams were carrying unsuspecting workers in their holiday attire; 'buses were crowded; and the streets of the poorer parts through which he passed were thronged with children. He caught glimpses of them in less busy thoroughfares, playing in the middle of the road, and at sight of them he caught his breath. They would go out, vanish, at a snap of a finger, all of them, every one of them. There would be none to mourn them—there was a comforting thought in that.

As he passed a hospital he saw what had evidently been the result of a street accident carried through the doors of the institution. All the thought, all the work, all the science which would be employed to bring back that battered wreck to life and health, would be wasted.

The wonderful inventions of man, the amazingly competent systems he had set up, would disappear with their inventors, and the history of mankind would end with all the history that mankind had written.

He could not understand it; he could not believe it.

His car skidded across the nose of a horse,

and its driver cursed him in voluble Cockney. He slowed his car down to apologize. The driver told him to go to hell. Jimmy grinned, and with a wave of his hand, went on.

His way lay across Westminster Bridge; and under the shadow of the great grey house, that monument to democracy and its power, he thought of all the men who had spoken within those walls. The Disraelis, Brights, Gladstone, Palmerston, Peel—shadows, and soon to be less than shadows. Who would remember them or know of them? Who was to perpetuate the fame of Billie Marks, that eminent theatrical lady whose portrait adorned the hoardings?

Only the insects and the fishes might survive the cataclysm, and, in the course of millions of years, produce all over again the beginning of a new civilization. And where London stood would be a great mound of earth, covered with forests, perhaps; and New New York City would be just the rocky platform of Manhattan Island; and when the winds had blown away the dust of crumbled masonry, and kindly nature had covered the desolation with her verdure, there would be a new America awaiting through the ages new discoverers, or equipping expeditions to locate a mythical Europe.

He was passing down Pall Mall, when a shrill whistle attracted his attention. He saw Ferdie's big motor-car parked in the centre of the road before he saw Ferdie standing on the steps of a club, beckoning him frantically.

Ferinand had gone to town an hour before him and he was the last person Jimmy expected to see. He pulled his car into the curb, and Ferdie walked along to him.

"Jimmy, old thing," he said, "I saw that bright lad this morning."

"Elmers?" asked Jimmy quickly.

Ferdie nodded.

"Spotted him in the Park. He was walking with a respectable old boy, and he was all shaved and dolled-up."

"What did you do?" asked Jimmy. "You know there's a warrant for him, and it is absolutely essential that he should be arrested?"

"That's what I thought," nodded Ferdie. "It also struck me that it would be a good idea to find out where he was living. Anyway, I might have lost him in the Park; it's a ticklish place to trail people in a 60 h.p. Italia. "Partly," he added unnecessarily, "because I've never taught the dashed thing to jump railings or swim lakes, and it looks as if I'm never goin' to," he added, with grim humour.

"Well, what did you do?" asked Jimmy, anxious to get off that subject.

"I followed him as slowly as the old 'bus could go. He was just about to turn into a house in Welton Street—that's just off Piccadilly—when he must have spotted me out of the corner of his eye, for he walked on. The stout gentleman went into the house, No. 16. The gent's name is Palythorpe—how's that for a piece of high-class detective work?"

"Palythorpe?" said Jimmy. "I wonder if the Prime Minister knows him? Come along with me, Ferdie; maybe you have done something useful before you die."

They found the Prime Minister at home. He had been up all night and looked less troubled and more serene than Jimmy had expected.

"Palythorpe?" he said quickly. "It can't

be that unspeakable blackguard—wait a moment."

He went out of the room quickly and returned in five minutes.

"Yes, it is evidently the same man," he said. "He owns a scurrilous weekly paper."

"But surely he wouldn't publish anything about this," said Jimmy, horrified at the thought. "What was the summary, sir?"

"It was a statement prepared by Maggerson and the Bishop setting out in as plain language as they could command, just what is going to happen. We prepared this, because there was a time when the Bishop wondered whether it would not be his Christian duty to give the world an opportunity for making spiritual preparations. But, mild as the statement was, it was too terrible to put into circulation; even the Bishop agreed to that."

"But what object could he have?"

"The man has been to prison, and I was responsible for sending him there," said the Prime Minister. "He had gone out of my mind until—last night. You remember I said there was a man."

"But such a statement would not hurt you, sir?" insisted Jimmy.

The Prime Minister shook his head.

"It would be enough for Palythorpe to know that I wish this secret kept. There is also the possibility that he might believe that it was a scare without any basis of reason, and publish the summary in order to throw ridicule on me—from whatever motive he put the summary into circulation the effect would be the same. Scientific men would recognize immediately that the statement told the truth. There would be a panic in this country, probably throughout the world, a panic of such a nature which I dare not let my mind contemplate. I've sent the police to arrest Palythorpe. Could you arrange to meet them at the corner of Welton Street? I told them that I should ask you to accompany them."

"Like a shot," said Ferdie, who had not been asked.

When they reached Welton Street the police car was already standing at the corner and four men were grouped near by. One of them must have known Jimmy, although the man was a stranger to him.

"If you'll show me the house, sir——"

Ferdie led the way, but their search was in vain. Mr. Palythorpe had gone out five minutes earlier, the servant told them.

One detective was left in charge of the flat to conduct a search, and Jimmy and his friend took the other three to the office of the little sheet which Palythorpe edited. Here too they drew blank. The office was closed and locked. It was a public holiday, and Mr. Palythorpe did not carry his enmity of the Prime Minister to such lengths that he had denied his employees their vacation. Probably his employees had had something to do with the matter.

The detectives had a consultation.

"Who prints this paper?"

One of them fished a copy from his pocket and examined the imprint.

"It says printed by Tyrhitt Palythorpe."

"Has he a press of his own?" asked Jimmy.

"I'm blest if I know," said the detective, "but we can easily find out."

It was some time before the necessary information was forthcoming. Palythorpe had apparently printed his own paper. His new venture was of a semi-private character, and was sold in a sealed envelope. As to the exact location of the works there was some confliction of evidence. On a day like this, when all the business houses were closed, it was almost impossible to get into touch with the people who could have supplied the information. Printer after printer was called by telephone at his private residence, and none could give any kind of direction. Neither the telephone book nor the London Directory carried the name of Mr. Palythorpe and his printing works.

It was a handicap to Jimmy that the police were not aware of the reason for the arrest and search. To them Palythorpe was a political offender of the first magnitude who had been guilty of some mysterious crime against the State, as to the exact character of which they were ignorant.

Jimmy had a short consultation with Ferdinand.

"Suppose he prints the information," said Ferdie. "I don't see what he can do with it. No trains are running. He couldn't distribute it to-day if he tried."

"There is a post," said Jimmy significantly, "and there is an early morning delivery. The postmen are the only people who are working to-morrow."

"But he couldn't get the news all over the country," protested Ferdie. "Do you suggest that he could get into touch with every lad in every village?"

Jimmy shook his head.

"It is only necessary that two of those summaries should go to every town. The news would be out in five minutes—and then!"

"He wouldn't do it," said Ferdie. "No man would be such an unutterable blackguard!"

But he did not know Mr. Tyrhitt Palythorpe.

CHAPTER EIGHTEEN

FIVE minutes after Ferdie had left the vicinity of Welton Street, Tom Elmers had joined his companion of the morning, and found him pacing his room nervously.

"Who was that?" he asked.

"A fellow named Ponter. He's a friend of Blake's. He chased me once out of Blake's garden."

"Did he recognize you?" asked Mr. Palythorpe quickly.

"Of course he did," snapped Tom.

Mr. Palythorpe's genial face was puckered in an expression of thought.

"Then the best thing we can do is to get away from here as quickly as we can," he said, diving for his hat. "This will mean bad trouble for me."

They found a wandering taxi, and Palythorpe gave him an address in Acton. Up a side street was the little printing-shop which the man had bought for a song after his release from prison, and was the foundation of his new activities.

It was no more than a grimy, dilapidated shed, with one press, and cramped accommodation for the half a dozen compositors whom he employed. In the language of the trade it was a "rat-house." Mr. Palythorpe employed only this type of labour, for reasons not unassociated with certain profitable sidelines which he ran. For he was a great printer of surreptitious lottery tickets and illegal sweepstake prospectuses.

He unlocked the discoloured door and ushered Elmers into the stuffy interior. Tom Elmers looked round with the supercilious contempt of one who had worked under ideal conditions in a well-conducted office.

"Not much of a ship!" he said.

"It's good enough for me," said Mr. Palythorpe shortly.

At one end of the building a small cubby-hole of an office had been run up.

"Come in here," said Palythorpe, switching on a light. "Now, let me have a look at this paper."

It had been Mr. Maggerson's boast that his summary was understandable to the meanest intelligence.

It is a reproach which has often been levelled against the scientist that he is the only man who has anything worth saying, and yet does not know how to say it. In this case, however clear the summary might be to him and to his friends, it had been more or less gibberish to Tom Elmers. Tom had been told to discover papers and bring them to his principal, and he had obeyed, but a perusal of the summary had disappointed him.

"It's about a comet," he said as he took it slowly from his pocket.

"About a comet?" repeated the other incredulously.

Tom nodded.

"I told you there wasn't much in it. Old Maggerson has been making calculations for days and days. I used to watch him through a hole in the floor."

Mr. Palythorpe was chagrined and displayed his disappointment.

"Then all they've been doing is making astronomical calculations," he said with a curse. "And I have wasted all my time. I thought there was a woman in it. But why was Van Roon killed? You don't know anything about that?"

Tom Elmers shook his head.

"Ask me another," he said sarcastically. "Here is the paper."

Mr. Palythorpe adjusted a pair of rimless glasses and began to read.

As he read Tom Elmers saw his face go white, and before he had finished, the hands which held the closely written sheets of manuscript were shaking.

"My God!" he breathed as he put the papers down.

"What's up?" asked Tom, alarmed.

Mr. Palythorpe did not answer him. He sat with his chin in his palm, staring at the discoloured blotting pad.

"He doesn't want anybody to know. That is it," he said aloud, though he was speaking to himself. "He doesn't want anybody to know! It would break his heart——"

He looked up suddenly. His eyes were narrowed and shone beyond the swollen lids bright and hard.

"It would break his heart," he said slowly. "By God, that's what I'm going to do! Get your coat off!"

"What's the idea?" asked Elmers in surprise.

"Get your coat off and go to that case. You'll find a couple of founts of pica type —I want you to set something."

Mr. Elmers did not display any enthusiasm.

"This is supposed to be a holiday," he said. "What's the idea? I've been working hard for you and all I get out of it is——"

"Do as you're told," snarled the man and, taking some paper from the rack, he began to write.

Tom Elmers had no intention of working that day and it was with the greatest reluctance that he slipped off his jacket, and rolling up his sleeves, sought for and found the cases of type which Palythorpe had indicated.

Presently the stout man came out and laid a sheet of paper in front of him.

"Set that," he said, and gave instructions as to the length and spaces between the lines. "Make it a twenty-six em line and double-lead it. I only want to fill one little page."

"Is this all that has to be set?" said Tom, brightening up.

Palythorpe nodded.

"While you're doing it I'll be addressing envelopes, and after you've finished you can come and help me. I have three thousand addresses and I think they'll do the trick."

Tom sniffed.

"All right," he said.

"No, by the Lord!" cried Palythorpe. "I've got over three thousand addressed envelopes ready for the next issue of the paper. They will do—they're pretty evenly distributed."

Tom did not answer. His eyes were staring at the first few lines of the copy:—

"To-day, May 16th, the world will come to an end at four-thirty-three Greenwich mean-time. The unnamed Comet which has been visible for three weeks will strike the earth at a point six hundred and thirty miles north of the south pole——"

He read the lines again and then turned to Palythorpe.

"What's this?" he asked huskily. "Are you putting up a scare?"

And then it was that Palythorpe made a mistake. He himself had read and accepted the news, if not with equanimity at least with courage.

"It is true," he said; "this is the gist of the summary you brought me. Now you understand why they've been working near the Observatory. . . ."

The steel "stick" in Elmers's hand dropped with a crash to the floor. He staggered back, his face livid.

"It's a lie, a lie!" he shrieked. "I tell you it's a lie!"

"It's true enough," said Palythorpe shakily, for some of the man's terror had communicated itself to him; and then, without warning, a raging lunatic leapt at him and gripped him by the throat.

"You're lying; you're trying to frighten me! The world is not coming to an end, you devil! You devil!"

Palythorpe struck out at the madman. Twice he hit the bloated face; and then, with superhuman strength, Elmers flung him away

and darted to the door. It was locked, but
he tugged at the handle, whimpering in the
high clear note which Jimmy had heard when
Stope-Kendrick came flying across Blackheath to his death. He released his hold of
the handle, and springing on to a bench,
kicked out the window and, struggling
through the broken glass, dropped into the
street.

A policeman saw the wild figure, his face
streaming with blood from the glass, and
sought to intercept him. Elmers flung him
aside and raced down the main street. An
empty taxi-cab was pulling away from a rank
and he leapt upon the running board.

"There, there," he said and pointed ahead.
"Go faster, faster, faster!"

The frightened driver tried to fling himself
from his seat, but Tom's hand gripped him
by the collar and wrenched him back.

"I'll kill you! I'll kill you!" he sobbed.
"Take me away from this, do you hear?"

"Where do you want to go?" gasped the
driver.

"To a church, any church . . ."

It was at a little Catholic Chapel of the

Sacred Heart, on the Barnet Road, that the sweating driver brought his car to a standstill; and Elmers, springing off before the taxi had stopped, flew up the steps and into the cool interior. A priest was standing near the altar-rails in the deserted church, giving directions to some workmen who were repairing the mosaic floor. He heard the clatter of the man's feet and faced him.

Elmers staggered up the aisle, his arms outflung, making a queer and eerie noise that momentarily turned the blood of the priest to ice.

For a second they confronted one another. The calm, the serene, frocked figure; the uncouth half-made printer.

Tom looked past him, and the priest saw the man's breast rising and falling and heard the shrill wail of mortal terror in his voice.

"Jesus! Jesus!" Tom Elmers's voice rose to a scream; and he stumbled forward and, gripping the altar cloth convulsively with his grimy hands, he fell.

And the world ended for him in that second.

CHAPTER NINETEEN

IT WAS dawn on the morning of the 16th and a big Rolls stood at the door of Blake's Priory.

Jimmy came out of the house, fastening his gloves, and cast an eye at the sky.

The chauffeur was waiting.

"I shall not want you, Jones," said Jimmy. "You had better go to your home and your people."

Jones grinned.

"I've got neither home nor people, sir," he said cheerfully; "and if I don't go with you I shall stay here."

"Well, you'd better come along," said Jimmy. "No, you'd better stay," he said, after a moment's thought.

It was curious how he had to readjust his system of conduct in the light of the great factor. He could not take the man with him, because that would mean Jones would have to be told, and he could not trust any man to receive that stunning news with philosophy.

Joe came out, buttoned to the neck in a heavy overcoat, for the morning was chilly; and then Delia came, and Jimmy took both her hands in his and smiled into her face.

"You look lovely, Delia," said Jimmy. "Did you sleep well?"

She nodded.

"It was absurd to sleep, wasn't it?" she laughed. "But one cannot break the habit of a lifetime, even though——"

She looked at Jones and cut her words short.

Joe climbed into the back of the car, lit his pipe and pulled a rug over his legs.

"Good-bye, Jones," said Jimmy.

"Good morning, sir," said Jones, walking by the side of the slowly moving car. "What time do you expect to come back? You'll be back to-night, of course, sir?"

"I don't think so," said Jimmy, and, with a wave of his hand, was gone.

He did not look back at Blake's Priory. This "Day of Uniting" was a day of looking forward.

The streets were deserted, the world was sleeping, and the only people he saw were the policemen slowly pacing their beats.

They stopped at Guildford for breakfast, and Guildford was *en fête*. "The Day of Uniting" coincided with the unveiling of the new War Memorial, and the streets were alive with holiday folk. Here, apparently, the instructions in the Proclamation were not being observed. Servants were on duty at the hotel where they breakfasted, though one of them told him that they were being released at twelve o'clock, to spend the day with their families.

The newspapers had been published that morning, since their publication did not involve working very far into "The Day." Jimmy bought a copy on the street and gazed at it with interest. In billions of years' time, perhaps, a new civilization would reach its zenith. Would there be brains that could understand, supposing their owners discovered a newspaper which had escaped the world's destruction and the passage of ages, just what all these little figures in black upon white signified to a bygone age?

He turned to the principal news page. There was a story of a crime which had been committed a week before and which had excited attention. There was a statement concerning a new measure for the adjustment of Income Tax which was to be introduced at the next session of Parliament; there were one or two speeches; and the record of a meeting of the Royal Society, where a Professor had lectured upon the peculiar properties which had been discovered in radio-active clay.

Jimmy folded the paper with a sigh and put it into his pocket.

"A very uninteresting newspaper," he said; "and thank God for it!"

"What did they do with this man Polythorpe?" asked the girl.

Jimmy shook his head.

"I think he has been sent to the Tower of London. It is very likely," he added simply, "that he is dead."

Their progress was a leisurely one. Jimmy had one hand on the steering-wheel, in the other he held Delia's. Her calmness was anodyne to his troubled spirit, and he mar-

velled at her serenity. She had extracted the
sting from death, and he worshipped her.

At a little village where they had stopped
they met the vicar outside the parish church,
and he gossiped pleasantly.

"Did you see the comet last night? I am
told it was a wonderful sight."

"No," said Jimmy. "I did not see it."

"Some of my parishioners saw it. The
men who went to work very early in the
morning. They said it was extremely beautiful, much larger than any comet they had
seen. In fact, it was visible after daybreak."

"How   fascinating!"   said   Jimmy   and
changed the subject.

They had to avoid the big military camp
which the Government had created on Salisbury Plain during the war, and at last they
came to a spot in a fold of land, where a little
stream trickled and trees cast a pleasant shade.

Jimmy sighted it from a distance and, turning the car from the road, brought it across
country into the tiny valley.

"And here we are," he said gently. "We'll
have lunch in a jiffy. I'm starving."

He and the girl set the cloth, whilst Joe

wandered off on to the Plain, and they talked of picnics and discussed food in "a perfectly animal way," said Delia apologetically.

Jimmy looked around. Joe was nowhere in sight.

"Delia, I haven't spoken to you about our marriage," he said. "When you came to me and—and asked me, you knew, didn't you?"

She nodded.

"And you wanted this to happen be-fore——"

She raised her grave eyes to his.

"I wanted just to know that you were mine," she said. "I wanted the spiritual union, the sense of belonging to you—I won-der if you understand?"

"I think I do," said Jimmy quietly. "You don't know what comfort these hours bring and how cheerfully I can face whatever comes because of that very union you spoke of."

He put his arm round her shoulders and drew her to him. For the second time in his life he kissed her, and he thought how lovely it would be if there were a to-morrow, and, wincing, put the thought from his mind.

Joe came back soon after. He was never a loquacious man; he had hardly spoken a word all the day.

"What are you thinking about, Joe?" asked Jimmy after the lunch was cleared away.

"Oh, just things," said Joe vaguely. "I wasn't thinking of this afternoon—except in a way. I was just hoping."

"Hoping? For what?"

Joe shook his head.

"I had a thought this morning as I was dressing. Just a pin-point thought, and it took me a long time before I could hold it for my own comfort."

"Pass it along," said Jimmy with a smile. "We all want a little comforting."

But Joe smiled and shook his head again.

"I think not," he said.

The morning was hot. The early part of the afternoon was sultry. On the southern horizon great cumulus clouds were piling up, and an occasional gust of wind ruffled the leaves of the tree under which they sat.

"A storm is coming up," said Jimmy. He

looked at his watch; it was half-past three.

"I hope it rains," said the girl. "I love rain."

For half an hour it seemed that the clouds did not move, and then the storm began to move with extraordinary rapidity. The white thunder-heads towered higher and higher, and the horizon was fringed with a purple haze. Presently they heard the low rumble of thunder.

"I think we'd better get into the car," said Jimmy. "Help me put up the hood, Joe."

They had it fixed and were in the car when the first few spots of rain fell. Almost immediately after, there was a blinding flash of light, and a crash that sent the girl shivering closer to Jimmy.

"It is only a storm, my dear," he smiled.

"I know—only my nerves are just a little —a little upset," she said faintly.

Jimmy had thought the storm would be a severe one and in this he was not mistaken.

The fitful wind strengthened to a steady gale. The rolling plains were rimmed with quick blue flashes of ribbon lightning. The thunder grew from a roll to a roar, and rose to an incessant crackle and crash.

And then the rain came down. It poured a solid sheet, blotting out all view of the Plain, and through it and above it the blue lightning went "flick-flick"! The air suddenly cooled and the twilight, which the forerunners of the storm brought, darkened to a terrifying gloom.

Delia pressed her face against Jimmy's breast and put her hands to her ears.

Suddenly there came a terrifying explosion, that deafened and stunned them. It was followed by a sound as though giant hands had torn a sheet of steel as men tear paper.

Jimmy drew the girl tighter and pulled a rug over her head and shoulders. He glanced at Joe Sennett. The old man was sucking at his pipe, his blue eyes fixed on vacancy.

"That must have been a tree that was struck," said Jimmy presently, glancing out and straining his head backward. "Yes," he nodded, "it was only a tree, Delia; and lightning, my darling, never strikes——"

A blue light so intensely brilliant that it

blinded him blazed suddenly before his eyes; an ear-splitting crash; and the car shook.

"In the same place," murmured Jimmy.

But he knew that it was the second of the trees which had been shattered, for he had seen a molten rivulet of liquid light running along the ground.

It seemed as though the pandemonium had lasted two hours. Then he looked at his watch. It was half-past four, and the storm was passing. Rain still fell, but it was lighter. He waited, every second an agony, his watch gripped so tightly in his hand that he broke the glass without realizing the fact. He looked down at the girl, and, miracle of miracles, she was asleep! Exhausted nature was taking its toll, and in the midst of that horrific moment, she had surrendered.

Jimmy uttered a prayer of thankfulness. He did not dare turn to Joe, for fear he should wake her; but presently he heard a movement behind him, and the old man bent over the back of the seat and looked down at the girl, and Jimmy saw a smile on his face.

They waited. How long Jimmy did not know. His senses were numbed, his mind a blank. Then suddenly the girl moved, opened her eyes, and sat up.

"I've been asleep," she said, aghast. "What is the time?"

Jimmy peered at his watch. It was a quarter after five! They looked at one another, and it was Joe Sennett who made the first move. He rose, opened the door of the car, and stepped out. The rain had ceased. Far away to the northward they saw the black bulk of the storm sweeping on its way, but above, the patches of blue between the cloud rack were growing bigger, and the sun, showing under the western edge of the cloud line, flooded the plains with golden splendour.

"I think we'll have some tea," said Jimmy huskily.

And when he looked at his father-in-law he found that Joe Sennett had already lighted the vapour stove they had brought with them.

A solemn trio they were. They sat on the running-board and sipped at their tea, each busy with his own thoughts. Presently the girl asked:

"What was in the telegram, Jimmy?"

"Telegram?" said Jimmy with a start.

"The telegram I brought over to you at the Warden's Lodge?"

Jimmy gaped at her.

"I never read it," he said. "Whatever made you think of it?"

She shook her head smilingly.

"Whatever makes one think of anything at any time?" she asked.

Jimmy realized that he was wearing the same suit of clothes that he had worn on the night he had been taken to the Warden's Lodge. He put his hand in his side pocket, without, however, discovering the telegram. It was in the inside breast pocket that he found it.

"Rather bulky, isn't it?" he asked as he tore it open.

There were three sheets and they were written in German. He looked hurriedly at the last page.

"Schaffer," he said with a groan. "And I don't understand a word——"

He heard the girl's laugh.

She took the pages from his hand and read them through, and he saw a frown gathering on her forehead and waited for her to speak.

When she did her voice was very shaky.

"I don't understand it quite," she said, "and yet——"

"Read it," said Jimmy.

She smoothed the folds of the sheets on her lap and began:

"It is addressed to you and reads: 'My letter to Van Roon was to point out four extraordinary inaccuracies in Maggerson's Calculus of Variations. These are obviously printer's mistakes, but unless they are immediately corrected, there will be grave and serious errors in all astronomical tables which are worked out from the calculus. Please see Maggerson and tell him. As an instance of the danger, I might tell him that I worked out parallax of the new Comet, and, according to his calculus, it would collide with the Earth on the 16th May, whereas is really crosses the Earth's orbit twenty-three days before the Earth reaches line of supposed contact. Schaffer."

It was Joe Sennett who spoke first.

"That was my thought," he said in a low voice.

"Did you know?"

"I only know that that dog Elmers deliberately tampered with the type of three books, and I could only pray that he had also done the same with Mr. Maggerson's Tables. It was a faint hope, but if he had, and had done the work so cleverly that it could not be detected at sight, then it was possible that Mr. Maggerson had made a great error."

Jimmy rose and stretched himself, and on his face dawned a smile which was a veritable smile of life.

"That is what happened," he said softly. "I know it; I know it!" And then he laughed, a long, low, hearty laugh that ended in something like a sob. He picked up the girl in his arms, kissed her and sat her in the car.

"Let us go back to life," he said as he cranked up, and the sunlight was still in the sky, though the stars were shining brightly overhead, when the mud-spattered Rolls turned into the drive of Blake's Priory, to the consternation of Mr. Jones, the chauffeur, who was entertaining a lady friend to supper in the dining-room.

THE END

www.ingramcontent.com/pod-product-compliance
Lightning Source LLC
Chambersburg PA
CBHW031003260626
47169CB00002B/682